A Cuckold's P

Jessie Sinclair

Copyright © 2017 Jessie Sinclair

All Rights Reserved

Contents

About The Author

Jessie is an erotica writer who loves everything about the world of femdom. She loves being in control of men and having them squirm under her feet. Her favorite topics to write about include foot fetishism, financial domination, chastity, tease and denial, ballbusting/CBT, and cuckolding. Her collections of stories are based from personal experience and her deepest, most exhilarating fantasies.

Author Central Page

Taken By Our Neighbor

Jessie Sinclair

Copyright © 2017 Jessie Sinclair

All Rights Reserved

Chapter 1

"Babe, be careful with that shelf, it was my grandma's, god rest her soul."

"Okay okay I'm trying! It weighs more than a freaking car!" I remarked to my wife, Justine.

Justine and I had just moved into this upscale California coastal neighborhood after I landed a hot new job at a local consulting company. It was a great gig and I got paid almost twice as much as my old job. And best of all, we used the signing bonus to buy our dream home.

"Well it would be much easier if you worked out more!" My wife said as she teased me in her skimpy blue bikini.

I mean I wasn't the most built guy, but I wasn't a fat slob as well. I tried my best to work out as often as I could.

"Alright, well just be careful with it. I'm going inside to make a drink. It's so hot out here." She said.

I put down the enormous shelf as I stepped out of our

moving truck. As I wiped the sweat from my face, I heard a deep, booming voice from my right.

"Hi there, you guys need help moving your furniture?"

I turned my head and saw an enormous black man. He must have been at least 6'5"; he was so tall it seemed like he could block out the sun.

His white teeth contrasted against his sleek ebony skin. To say this man was muscular would be an understatement. He looked like a lean NFL football player. He wore nothing but a pair of board shorts and flip flops.

Before I could say anything my wife responded lighting fast.

"Yes, that would be great. My husband, Chris has a bad back so he can't lift too much." She said with a smile on her face.

I saw Justine checking out this Greek god's abs. They looked like solid stone that had been chiseled into a masterpiece.

The man laughed before formally introducing himself. "Hi, I'm DeMarco. I'm your neighbor; I live in the house right over there." He pointed with his giant finger at the nice house to the left of us.

"Hi DeMarco, I'm Justine." She said, almost blushing at this handsome black man.

DeMarco shook her hand and kissed it like a gentleman. She giggled at his gesture. I was a bit embarrassed that my wife was flirting with this incredible hunk, but even I had to admit he was good looking.

"Chris, nice to meet you." DeMarco said as he extended his hand out to me. We shook and I could almost feel his vice grip crush every single bone in my hand. The guy was a strong as a gorilla and didn't seem to know his own strength.

DeMarco took a look in the truck and saw that it was half full. He quickly took every piece of furniture out of the truck with little effort.

DeMarco moved all of our furniture without breaking a bead of sweat. He flexed his muscles with every movement. Justine seemed infatuated with this man. Before we knew it, DeMarco had already moved our furniture inside.

Don't get me wrong, I appreciated his help, but I just didn't like how the guy flirted with my wife right in front of me.

Before DeMarco could leave, Justine asked if he wanted anything to drink.

DeMarco looked at his watch before politely declining my wife's offer. "I've got to get started on my barbecue. I'm having a few of the neighbors over. You guys should totally come over and meet everyone if you're not too busy."

"Oh that sounds like a lot of fun, we'll definitely be there!" Justine said, without even consulting me.

"Great, I'll see you guys there in like half an hour."

DeMarco left our house and Justine seemed to be fixated on his ass as he walked away.

"Hey, I thought we were going to the movies tonight?" I

said to my wife.

"Oh, I totally forgot about that. Well this sounds like more fun anyways. Besides we should get to know our neighbors."

I was reluctant to go to DeMarco's party. I already knew Justine had a big crush on him and it made me a bit insecure. As we arrived, it turned out to be a small little gathering.

DeMarco had a few tables set up around his pool. There were a few of the neighborhood kids running and jumping around.

"Hey guys!" DeMarco's face lit up as he saw us. He introduced us to everyone around the block. Everyone at the party seemed to be pretty nice, but I just couldn't get over at how the guy would flirt with my wife.

I mean I bit my tongue because I didn't to sound petty, but it really bothered me. As I ate a hamburger, I could hear Justine laugh at one of his jokes.

All of a sudden everyone at the party began to chant, "Cannon Ball! Cannon Ball! Cannon Ball!"

"Uh what's going on?" I said as I leaned over to ask DeMarco.

"Oh it's nothing; we usually have a cannon ball diving contest with everyone here. It's kind of like our little tradition. Winner gets to take home the leftovers."

"Oh that sounds like fun!" Justine said. "Let's do one together, Chris!"

"Oh no, I can't I just ate. I should probably wait a bit before going into the water."

Justine pouted. "Oh come on! Don't be a party pooper!"

"Well..." I said, contemplating the decision.

Before I could make up my mind, DeMarco just had to butt in. "Oh that's okay. I'll do one with you." He said as he carried her off.

Justine had the time of her life being carried in DeMarco's muscular arms. He carried her onto the diving board and they jumped off together as she screamed in excitement.

"Oh my god!" Justine said while giggling. The force of
their crash caused the water to splash the front row audience as
everyone clapped and cheered at the performance.

The party died out after another hour and we took home the
leftovers as everyone seemed to love Justine's and DeMarco's
performance.

I couldn't wait to get out of there. As we lay in bed
before going to sleep, Justine just couldn't stop smiling. "Hey
wasn't that so much fun today?" She remarked.

"Uh yeah, I guess." I wasn't too happy with how DeMarco
flirted with my wife. I was too afraid to confront her about it
though.

As I turned to turn off our light, Justine attacked me with
her lips all of a sudden. We kissed with such passion not seen
since our honeymoon.

Without saying a word, Justine straddled me. She reached
back and grabbed my hard cock, lining it up with her dripping
wet pussy.

She slid up and down on my member; my cock glided in with ease. A faint whimper escaped my wife's lips. I was completely flabbergasted. I couldn't believe how horny she was.

Her moans got louder and louder. We fucked like wild animals in the dark that night. We didn't speak while we made love, but I had a feeling she was thinking about DeMarco drilling her pussy. For the first time that day, I didn't mind DeMarco being in my wife's thoughts...

Chapter 2

We saw DeMarco several more times this week. We saw him at the park...we saw him when we got our mail...we saw him at the grocery store.

And every single time we saw him, he would flirt with my wife. And every night after we saw DeMarco, Justine would be incredibly horny.

Like clockwork, my wife would climb on top of me until she came. She would close her eyes and moan softly.

One time I thought I even heard her moan DeMarco's name. I had the sneaking suspicion that she was fantasizing about him.

At first I was upset about it, but I knew Justine loved me and would never cheat. Plus, all that pent up passion was passed onto me. We never had a more vibrant sex life until we moved here.

The next day my afternoon meeting was canceled and I rushed home. I wanted another piece of the hot and steamy love making session Justine and I had last night.

I didn't text Justine as I wanted to surprise her. I pulled into our garage and saw her car there. Perfect, she was home!

As I walked past our white wooden gates I could hear Justine giggling.

"Oh my god! You're so naughty! No, I don't think we should do that." She said while trying to suppress her laughter.

"Why not?" The booming voice responded. Wait a minute...I recognized that voice! It was DeMarco!

I quickly walked to the wooden fence that separated our front and back yards.

What I saw completely surprised me. My wife was in the backyard tanning in a skimpy pink bikini that barely covered her intimates. Meanwhile, DeMarco sat next to her with a bottle of sunscreen in his hands.

"The neighbors could see us and tell Chris. Besides, you know I'm married, DeMarco."

That didn't stop this handsome black man from squirting a handful of sunscreen onto his large bear paws. He rubbed it around his palms to warm up the lotion.

"Don't worry, no one will find out. Besides, you wouldn't want to get sun-burnt, would you?"

"Well...I guess not..." Justine said, unsure of herself.

DeMarco went ahead and placed his dominating hands all over my wife. He started with her upper back and moved his way down. His dark skin contrasted heavily against my wife's porcelain white skin.

Justine moaned softly as this Greek god graced her body. I was completely speechless as events unfolded. If I hadn't witness this scene I wouldn't have believed it.

I guess I could have called them out through the fence, but for some reason I didn't. It was a mix of fear, confusion, and...oddly enough very erotic.

I couldn't describe it...but it was hot watching this black man place his hands all over my wife.

I watched as DeMarco took things further step by step. Justine wasn't even resisting at this point.

DeMarco focused his hands on her legs now. He massaged every crevice of her body. It was weird...but I was actually starting to get hard in my pants.

After rubbing her back from top to bottom, our black neighbor unzipped Justine's bikini top. His large hands groped her supple, firm breasts.

Justine gasped in pleasure. "Oh...." She moaned.

A devious smile flashed across DeMarco's face. He knew his foreplay was successfully seducing Justine.

He got even more confident. DeMarco moved his right hand all the way down to her panties. DeMarco grabbed her firm ass, squeezing it like he would an apple.

"Oh!" Justine moaned once more. This time it was louder than the last one.

She spread her legs wider as DeMarco fondled her.

"Slap my ass." She whispered to him.

What? Slap her ass? She never asked me to do that!

DeMarco laughed; his personality all of a sudden turned even more dominant. "You know, you little white whores are always the kinkiest."

Our black neighbor pulled Justine's panties down, revealing her toned ass to the world. DeMarco obliged her request and held his hand up and swatted down, making contact with her bare ass.

The cracking sound of his hand against her flesh echoed towards me. My dick all of a sudden became fully erect, pushing against the fabric of my pants.

DeMarco slapped my wife's ass again and again and again. At this point, she was moaning louder and louder. I was afraid our other neighbors would decide to investigate the noise.

"Oh god!" Justine moaned. I saw that DeMarco had brought his finger tips to her pussy. He was finger fucking my wife!

Meanwhile, his left hand groped her breasts and flicked her nipples. I could tell Justine was having the time of her life. She never seemed this turned on when we were in bed.

"Oh yeah you want my thick fingers bad, don't you, cunt?"

"Oh yeah! Your fingers are bigger than my husband's dick." Justine said between her labored breathing.

My cock leaked precum in my pants as Justine took a joking shot at me.

"Oh god! I'm so close!" Justine announced.

"Cum for me, bitch!" DeMarco bellowed. "Cum for me and I might let you taste my cock!"

"Oh god! I'm cumming!" Justine shrieked at the top of her lungs. DeMarco took his spare hand and placed it on her lips to muffle the sound. No doubt he didn't want anyone to hear their fun.

At this point I had enough. Even though I was oddly turned

on, I couldn't let my wife be fucked by our neighbor...even if
he was a handsome, giant black man.

     I walked up to our door with the keys in my hand. I paused
for a minute. I didn't even have a game plan. I mean what would
I do? I wouldn't be able to stand toe to toe with DeMarco if it
came down to a physical confrontation.

     I decided it didn't matter, I just had to intervene to save
my manhood. I opened the door and ran for the backyard...

Chapter 3

As I made it to the backyard, my wife and DeMarco had already disappeared. All of a sudden I heard giggles coming from the upstairs bedroom.

"Oh DeMarco, you're so naughty!"

It was Justine! She brought him up to our bedroom? This was crazy!

I ran up the stairs and saw our bedroom door half open.

"Oh yeah, you want my big black cock, don't you?"

"Yes! I want to suck on it!"

I couldn't believe what I was hearing. I took a peek past the door and saw DeMarco standing at the edge of our bed. Meanwhile, Justine was kneeling on the bed, begging to suck our black neighbor's cock!

DeMarco waved his cock in front of her as Justine's eyes followed in a hypnotic rhythm.

"That's a good slut. Ooopen wiiide! I want you to take all 11 inches!"

11 inches?! That was crazy! DeMarco was twice as big as me! I couldn't believe my wife would want to deep throat a cock that big.

Justine graciously opened her mouth and DeMarco rammed his cock into her mouth. He wasn't even gentle.

My wife ran the tip of her tongue on his large cock. DeMarco was so huge, I could have mistaken him for a horse!

She swirled her tongue around his head like she was licking an ice cream cone. She took the entire massive cock into her mouth and deep throated his entire member.

I stepped into the room and froze for a second before speaking.

"Justine?...What are you doing?"

Justine and DeMarco turned around. His cock fell out of her

mouth with an audible pop.

Justine was silent for a moment before she collected her thoughts. "Hi babe....I was just um...having some fun with DeMarco.

DeMarco smiled. "Yeah, we were just having a little bit of fun. No hard feelings, right?"

"Sorry babe, I just had to have him. He was so muscular, so handsome, and just so sexy."

There wasn't even a hint of remorse to my wife's tone of voice.

"Really? You've never felt more satisfied?"

"I don't know...there's just something about him."

"Oh don't worry," DeMarco chimed in, "I've seen this all the time. Bored housewife just wants to experience black cock for the first time."

"You're not mad are you?" Justine said calmly.

"Um...I g-guess not. I mean if he makes you feel that way..."

"Just sit down and watch." DeMarco commanded me. He pulled up a chair to the side of the bed so I could watch him defile my wife.

I was in no position to stop what was about to happen. My wife and our black neighbor were going to have sex whether I wanted it or not.

I sat down as commanded while DeMarco focused his attention to my wife again.

"No where were we? Oh yeah...you were sucking on my big black cock you cunt! Open your mouth!"

Justine opened her mouth and DeMarco shoved his over sized penis into her mouth.

"You love my cock don't you!"

"Ggghh!" Justine choked on his large cock as she tried to

respond. I couldn't believe she could deep throat such a big object.

Apparently Justine wasn't sucking hard enough. DeMarco grabbed the back of her head for leverage and began fucking her mouth thoroughly.

"Mggh! Oh! Mhhh!" Justine groaned and moaned as DeMarco fucked her mouth and throat.

Our big black neighbor was using my wife as a sex toy and I was just sitting there...with a hardon in my pants. It was like a live porn scene in our bedroom.

"You want my cum in your whore mouth, don't you?!"

Justine nodded vigorously while her answer was muffled by his cock.

"Oh I bet you do! But not now. I want to fuck stretch out your tight pussy!"

DeMarco pulled his cock out of her mouth and forcibly flipped Justine on her back.

"Beg for my cock!"

I sat on the edge of the chair as DeMarco readied his cock for my wife's pussy. I noticed he wasn't wearing a condom, but luckily Justine was on birth control.

"Please DeMarco, I need your cock in me! I've never had one so big, please fuck me senseless!"

It was weird hearing my wife beg for another man's cock, let alone our neighbor.

"That's what I like to hear you whore!"

DeMarco positioned himself on top of Justine and mounted his cock. Her pussy lips were red and swollen from all the teasing.

Our black neighbor lowered the bulbous black head of his cock against her clit. Justine moaned in response. Justine leaned her head back as she bit down on her lips and flicked her nipples.

DeMarco slipped his cock into my wife's pussy with much more ease than I anticipated. I guess she must have been really wet. My dick dripped in my pants as DeMarco entered her.

DeMarco slid all the way in, slowly at first until his balls rested against her ass. My wife was moaning uncontrollably at his point.

He pulled out very slowly until only the tip was still inside. Next, DeMarco slammed his cock hard back in. The force of his trust sent vibrations to Justine's sensitive clit as she moaned and screamed.

"Oh god! You're so big DeMarco!"

All he could do was chuckle. Meanwhile, I was getting so turned on I was practically massaging my member against my pants.

"Oh fuck me! Fuck me! Fuck me DeMarco!"

"Oh I love it when you beg, whore!"

"Oh god!"

DeMarco trust his cock back in forth in my wife's pussy. He leaned forward and sucked on her nipples. He flicked them with his tongue and Justine nearly lost it as she came on his big hard dick.

"Oh god! I just came!"

Justine's body convulsed as she shook uncontrollably. She bit down on her lips as DeMarco defiled her sensitive pussy.

"I'm going to STRETCH your little white pussy!"

"Oh!!"

"I'm going to fill your dirty whore pussy with my cum!"

"Oh yes! Yes! Please!"

"You ready for my load?!"

"Yes DeMarco! I want it so bad! I want your warm load in me!"

"Well here it comes you slut!"

DeMarco placed both hands on the bed next to Justine's shoulders. He picked up the speed of his thrusts.

DeMarco's monster balls slapped vigorously against my wife's ass with every thrust. I couldn't believe how hard he was fucking her. I was afraid he would split Justine in half.

Justine screamed in pleasure as DeMarco rammed his cock in.

"Okay, here it comes!"

I looked back and saw DeMarco's leg tighten up. He grunted and let out a moan, signaling his climax.

I saw my wife's eyes open with great anticipation. She felt wave after wave of his hot cum erupt in her pussy.

"Oh god!"

The sensation of DeMarco's hot cum caused Justine to orgasm again. DeMarco pulled out of her pussy before his orgasm subsided.

"I want to drench you in my cum, whore! I own you and your pussy!"

He jerked his cock off and cum flew all over her chest and boobs.

In the end, DeMarco marked my wife as his property. Justine lay on the bed panting hard.

"Oh god, DeMarco...that was so amazing!"

"Glad you enjoyed it...both of you." He looked back at my hardon and smiled.

"Why don't you have your husband clean your creampie pussy for me."

Justine looked at me and I nodded. I knew what she wanted. I moved forward and crawled on the bed. I lowered my mouth and stuck my tongue out. I lapped up DeMarco's super sperm. I couldn't believe I tasted another man's cum.

DeMarco chuckled and put on his clothes again.

"Just let me know when you want to get drilled by my big cock again." He said while leaving.

Justine moaned in response to his command. Meanwhile I moved up and kissed my wife on the lips. We share our big black neighbor's cum.

"How did it feel?" I asked Justine.

"Oh god...it was so amazing. I've never felt anything like it."

Justine and I cuddled together after that weird experience. We passed out soon after that, but we both knew that would not be the last we would see of DeMarco...

Celebrity Cheat List

Jessie Sinclair

Copyright © 2017 Jessie Sinclair

All Rights Reserved

Chapter 1

"So, honey who would be on your list?"

"Huh? What?"

I had just stowed our luggage in the overhead bins on the plane when my wife, Julie, asked me something. I sat down in our first class cabin and closed the door.

Julie and I were flying from Miami to the Bahamas for a romantic holiday weekend getaway. It was a real posh resort that attracted many celebrities including a few well-known Hollywood actors.

"Come on Clark! I was saying who would be on your celebrity cheat list?"

"What's that?" I said, as I took a sip of the fine wine the stewardess had left on our table. I looked across at my wife who seemed more intrigued about this "cheat list."

"You know your celebrity cheat list? A list of celebrities you would get a hall pass to cheat on your spouse with."

"Oh, I don't know. That sounds so crazy, where in the world did you get that idea? And it's not like it'll ever happen."

"I read it on some Cosmopolitan article. Don't be so silly, honey, it's just a fun game to think about. The girls at the country club and I were discussing it earlier in the week."

Oh great...Cosmopolitan. That site had been a thorn in my side for the better part of my marriage. Those people have put some crazy ideas in my wife's head like how going without sex for a week can be beneficial to your health or why you should go vegetarian.

I hated that publication and I knew no good would come from this conversation.

"Well who would yours be?"

"Well I don't know...I hadn't thought about it too much. Probably no one, I just want you. Who was on your list?" I buttered up my response to Julie. I knew she would dig it and score me some brownie points for when I wanted to golf later next week.

"Well now you're just trying to make me feel bad!" Julie playfully slapped me across from her seat. "Well...I only had one on my list."

"Really? Who would that be?"

"Jerome Baldwin! He's soooo dreamy! I love his incredible six pack and the way he talks!"

I should have known. My wife idolized Jerome. He was the epitome of Hollywood fame and fortune. The guy stared in more billion dollar blockbusters than any actor in history. Jerome sure did have the life most could only dream of: fame, fortune, and more women than he could ever fuck.

I have seen his movies on more than one occasion on the part of Julie dragging us to the theaters for opening night. The guy was handsome, don't get me wrong, but I knew Julie wouldn't have a winter's chance in hell to land Jerome. It was just fun and wishful thinking.

"Oh, I guess that's not a surprise. I think we've seen every one of his movies. Anyways, isn't he married?"

"So what? Candice is so hot; I'd have sex with her too!"

Candice was Jerome's younger counterpart and a supermodel of ungodly assets if you know what I mean. I would often fantasize about her with my buddies at work.

"So, what do you think about the idea?"

"What idea?"

"You know...the hall pass. I get to jump Jerome's bones if it ever got that far."

At this point, I was wondering if the stewardess had slipped something into Julie's wine. I guess that's what reading too much Cosmo did to a girl.

"Well alright, you get a hall pass with Jerome." I said with a smile on my face. "Okay I think that's enough games for now. Let's talk about tonight; where do you want to go? I was thinking we could go out to dinner or maybe a walk on the beach."

"Well, I was thinking we should..." Julie began droning on and on about the plans she had for the night. We would probably land at the airport at around 8:30 PM, so we settled on getting some food and drinks at the resort bar.

The flight was short and before we knew it, we were on the tarmac again. An hour later, we had checked into the hotel and were ready to go check out the bar across from the lobby.

By the time we arrived at the bar, most of the other patrons had already left for the night. There were only about two or three other couples around.

"So, ready to order?" I asked my wife.

"Yeah I'm starving!"

Julie and I ordered beer, a side of chicken wings, and a tuna salad to share.

As we were talking, Julie brought up a familiar topic. "So, are you sure you don't have a celebrity crush?"

"Well...I guess I..."

Before I could even finish my sentence, Julie gasped. "Oh my god! Look who it is!" She pointed behind me.

I turned around and saw him...Jerome Baldwin! He was wearing a pair of beige shorts and a white t-shirt. On his arm was Candice, his busty blonde model wife. The pair looked like they had just arrived at the hotel.

"Oh wow, that's crazy. I guess he's vacationing here too."

"Wow I love what Jerome did to his hair? I didn't know he got a haircut!" Julie loved to gossip so the news of some Jerome new hairdo interested her greatly. "We should totally invite them over!"

"What? Don't be crazy, babe! They're freaking celebrities! They probably want nothing to do with us."

"Oh don't be such a negative Nancy; Jerome loves spending time with his fans! Stay here, I'm going to go talk to them."

Before I could stop her, Julie jumped out of her seat and headed straight for Jerome and his hot wife. From the distance,

I could see their reactions.

My wife approached them like they were old friends or something. The couple seemed to be receptive of her advances.

Julie pointed in my direction as Jerome whispered something into his wife's ear. And before I knew it, Julie was walking back with a big smile and Jerome and his wife in tow...

Chapter 2

"Honey! Jerome said he'd love to eat with us tonight! Can you believe it!?" Julie seemed like a schoolgirl in the presence of the celebrity power couple.

"Hi, I'm Jerome." The man needed no introduction as he extended his hand out.

"H-hi Jerome. I'm Clark, Julie's husband."

"Hi Clark." Candice said with a smile as she hugged me. I smelled her signature perfume emanating from her neck as we embraced quickly.

"So oh my god, we are your biggest fans, Jerome!" Julie was absolutely gushing at the man before us. Even I had to admit Jerome looked much more handsome in person.

Even though he was wearing a shirt, I could tell he was well built. He probably had another part in some action movie. Candice was no slouch either. She was dressed to kill in a blue summer dress.

Jerome and Candice were surprisingly friendly for celebrities. We talked and gossiped like old friends. They even let us take pictures together. The guys at work probably wouldn't believe I met Candice if I didn't have the pictures to back up the claim.

Hours went by and we drank together. We probably did three rounds of whiskey in a short period of time. The tone of the conversation suddenly began to become more serious.

"So what brings you two to the Bahamas?" My wife asked them.

"Oh, we're just vacationing because we haven't been able to spend much time together." Candice said as she took a sip from her margarita.

"You know, we were just talking about you on our flight here." Julie said with a smile on her face.

"Oh really? What did you talk about?" Jerome asked.

"Well, I don't think we should discuss that." I said with an embarrassing smile. I knew the direction Julie was headed in.

All of a sudden I felt Julie's heel connect with my shin for a sharp and quick strike. "Don't be silly honey. They'll find it hilarious!"

"What what is it?" Candice said. She seemed intrigued.

"Well, have you ever heard of the celebrity cheat list?"

"Oh my god! I was just reading it last week in Cosmo!"

"So, let me guess, I'm your celebrity cheat." Jerome said with a confident look on his face.

"How did you know?" Julie said with almost a surprise to her voice.

"Let's just say we've broken up a lot of marriages." He said with a confident, yet humble tone of voice.

"Wait...so you've actually taken a girl like that before?" Julie was practically on the edge of her seat.

I was worried now. I knew what she was trying to get at.

Candice and Jerome looked at each other for a moment before nodding. She took a sip of her drink. "Well, seeing as how we're both on vacation I guess we could have some fun." Candice had an irresistible smirk on her face.

Jerome carefully stroked Julie's hands while Candice licked her lips for me to see.

"W-what did you have in mind?" Julie and I said at the same time.

"Well I say you two come up to our room and find out."

Julie and I looked at each other in complete disbelief.

"Yes, let's go." My wife quickly replied as she stood up.

Jerome and Candice chuckled at Julie's enthusiasm. "Say, Clark...why don't you bring up as a bottle of wine. Choice is yours; just put it on our tab. It would let us get to know your lovely wife better."

I couldn't believe what I heard from Jerome. I felt uneasy

leaving Julie with Jerome, but Candice whispered dirty things
into my ear.

"Bring back a nice bottle of wine and I'll show you things
you've never experienced." She whispered seductively in my ear.
Her sultry voice caused my cock to jump in my pants.

"Yeah...u-um that sounds great. I'll...I'm uh going to uh
get a bottle of wine."

Before I knew it, superstar and A-list actor took off with
my wife and Candice to their penthouse suite. As I approached
the bartender, I saw Jerome's arms reach down and grope my
wife's ass.

"So, what can I help you with?" The bartender said,
snapping me out of my trance.

I picked out the most expensive bottle of wine on the list
since it was on Jerome's tab. It was over $2,000 for the thing
so be good.

I decided to order a beer as well, to let things simmer
upstairs. After a 10 or 15 minutes, I headed for the elevators.

Chapter 3

I walked up to Jerome's room; the door was unlocked. As expected, the penthouse suite was absolutely extravagant. Faint moans could be hard through the double doors to the bedroom.

I put my ear against the door. "Oh Jerome! I love how big your cock is!"

"That's what they all say honey!"

"How do you like the taste?"

"It's amazing! I've never had anything like it before."

I heard some loud sucking noises and could only assume what was going on inside. I couldn't handle it anymore; I had to find out what was going on.

I pried open the door and found Jerome Baldwin lying on the bed. My wife was on her knees between his legs giving him a killer blowjob. Meanwhile, he was making out with Candice. So this is how Hollywood celebrities live it up huh?

"Wow, you guys didn't waste any time." I said nervously.

"Clark! Come watch!" Candice said happily.

My wife was busy bobbing up and down on Jerome's monster black cock. It must have been at least 12 inches long. It put my member to shame for sure.

I quickly stripped down, wanting to get in on this hot action.

"Whoa there cowboy, what do you think you're doing?" Jerome said. Julie pulled her head up to look at me.

"Well, I was going to join in on the fun."

"Honey, we um..." Julie was cut off my Jerome.

"Here's the thing Clark. Candice and I love taking a man's wife for ourselves. We love to cuckold him. It's our 'thing'."

"Wait...what?"

If I heard Jerome correctly, he just said he was going to

ravish my wife and I wouldn't be getting any?

"Oh don't look so disappointed." Candice tried to console me. She dragged the tip of her index finger down on my chest until her hands rested on my hard cock. "You're going to get plenty of fun, just no penetration."

Candice bit down on her lip and let me see her glistening red pussy. It was one of the natural wonders of the world.

"Well...I guess I could live with that," I said as Candice hypnotized me with her pussy.

"Great, let's get back to it. Suck on my cock again, slut." Jerome ordered my wife.

Julie popped his cock back into her mouth. Meanwhile, Jerome sat back down against the pillows as Candice straddled his mouth with her pussy.

"Oh yeah! Suck on that pussy!"

Jerome darted his tongue in and out like a madman. It drove Candice absolutely insane. If only the guys could see what I saw; their brains would melt too!

"Kiss me baby!" Candice looked up at me with a devious smile.

She didn't need to ask me twice. I sat down over Jerome's firm chest and locked lips with this supermodel. From behind, Julie slapped my ass in approval.

"I need your cock." Julie said to Jerome. The look on her face was of pure bliss. My wife couldn't believe she was about to fuck her celebrity crush. I don't know if it was the alcohol or if it I somehow got caught up in the moment, but I wanted Julie to have him. I wanted her to enjoy it all and have the night of her dreams.

"Yeah? You want my big cock?" Jerome bellowed over his wife's pussy. "Fuck it then, you'll never have anything like it!"

My wife positioned herself above Jerome's massive black cock. "Hold his cock for me honey."

I parted lips with Candice and held the base of Jerome's

cock in my hand. My fingers barely wrapped around his warm flesh.

"Suck on his cock to wet it first." Candice hissed from behind me.

My wife chuckled at her order.

"Yeah, suck on it for me babe. I want it nice and wet for my tight pussy!"

I lowered my lips while maintaining eye contact with my beautiful wife. Meanwhile, Candice reached behind and grabbed my balls softly and rolled them around in her hands.

"Oh yeah, I love how big your balls are." She squeezed them slightly before jerking off my dick slowly while her husband continued to eat out her pussy.

I lowered my lips until I finally kissed the head of Jerome's cock. "How does it taste honey?"

"Much better than I expected."

Julie giggled at my comment. I wrapped my lips around the bulbous head and did my best to get Jerome off. I wasn't as good as my wife, but I heard him moaning below. She played with her pussy, anticipating this monster cock penetrating her.

After a few minutes of sucking and licking, my wife had enough. Julie just wanted that cock. She practically pushed me off. "Oh yeah! I've always dreamed about this!"

She inserted his cock in and slowly lowered herself all the way down so their hips met. His cock completely penetrated her pussy.

"I love how big you are!"

Julie began rocking back and forth on his cock. Jerome helped by thrusting up as well. I could hear the sweet harmony of their bodies smacking against each other.

Candice wrapped her lips around the side of my neck and made her way to my ear. "Suck on her clit," She whispered seductively to me like the devil.

I lowered myself down on Jerome's abs and kissed my wife's

clit. "Oh! That's the spot! Don't stop!"

At this point, whenever Jerome thrust up, his cock would graze against my tongue.

Both of them moaned in pleasure. Unexpectedly, Candice leaned forward and grabbed my cock from behind. She pulled it backward and teased the tip with her fingers.

"How does that feel?"

"Mmm!" I moaned loudly in response. My attention never wavered from the task at hand. I was giving my wife the best head she ever had.

"I'm going to cum in your pussy!"

"Give it to me! I want your warm cum!" Julie shrieked.

I just noticed that Jerome was fucking my wife without any protection! It was a good thing she was on birth control.

"Are you ready?!"

"Yes! Cum in me! I want it all!"

"Here it comes!" Jerome grunted loudly and I felt his muscles tighten from below me. His cock pulsed uncontrollably while my wife climaxed as well.

I kept sucking on her clit without any break. Jerome's warm cum gushed into my wife's pussy like a geyser. The cum began dripping out of her pussy as his orgasm subsided.

"Oh my god! That was so amazing!" My wife was panting like a dog as she dismounted Jerome's monster cock.

"I need some of that in me too!" Candice said, as she pushed me aside and scissored my wife. Their pussies mingled together over our legs. Jerome and I just laid back and enjoyed the show.

"So was this your first experience swinging?" Jerome said as he looked over at me.

"Yeah, it was amazing."

"So Clark, are you ready for your surprise?"

"What is it, Candice?"

The supermodel and my wife stopped scissoring each other and spread their legs wide. "You get to clean one of our pussies." The smile on her face turned me on.

I had to pick Candice. I could lick my wife's pussy any time. "I'm going to take yours."

"Come lick it then." She coaxed me.

My wife laughed as she moved in the opposite direction to make out with Jerome. I kissed Candice's red pussy lips like it was the last thing I would ever do. I tasted the sweet nectar from Jerome's cock. I lapped up his sperm like a good cuckold.

The four of us had much more fun until the wee hours of Sunday morning until we all collapsed on each other out of exhaustion. The trip was over before we knew it. Jerome and Candice kissed us goodbye later that afternoon.

"Here's our card, don't be a stranger if you're ever in LA." Candice said with a smile. She lightly slapped my cock.

Meanwhile, Jerome fingered my wife's raw pussy as he kissed her goodbye.

Julie and I headed back to the airport in complete glee. "So babe, was it as good as you expected?"

"Oh, it was so much better! I'm glad we had the talk before we arrived."

"Yeah, what a coincidence."

"So, who else do you have on your cheat list?" I asked her.

"Well...maybe Peter Jones."

"Really?"

"Yep."

"Well, I hope we run into Peter Jones soon as well. Maybe Jerome and Candice know him..."

Julie and I laughed our way back to the airplane as it took off. This was the cap to an unforgettable weekend.

Taken By My Boss

Jessie Sinclair

Copyright © 2017 Jessie Sinclair

All Rights Reserved

Chapter 1

"Hey babe, what do you want to do for dinner tonight?"

I walked into the kitchen to see my wife doing the dishes. She dried off her hands and began about her day.

"Oh hey, Josh. You'll never believe what happened to me today."

"What happened?"

"I ran into your boss, DeMarcus at the grocery store. We had a good time together."

"Yeah, I doubt that." I said under my breath. It was no secret I despised my boss.

My wife, Christine, didn't appreciate how I interrupted her. She flashed me a nasty glare and began telling her story again.

"Anyways, he took me out to coffee. He mentioned he would be staying at a hotel because his house was flooded. It'll be a week or so before he can move back in."

"Oh yeah?" My eyes lit up. It served that fucker right. That guy made me work late the other night so I couldn't make it home until 11:00 PM.

"Yeah, I felt bad for him so I invited him to say for us for the next week."

My heart nearly sank out of my chest. "You did what?!"

Christine continued to wash the dishes and ignored my obvious discomfort.

"Why did you invite him over? You know I don't like him!"

"Well I thought it would be nice to have him over. Now he'll owe you one. Plus he is your boss after all. It wouldn't hurt you to be nicer to him."

"Nicer to him? That guy is always a dick to me."

Christine finished up with the last of the dishes. I could smell something cooking already in the oven. She dried off her hands and put them on her nips.

"Honestly, Josh, I don't know what you're talking about. He's always very gentleman-like around me."

"Ugh, that's because he probably wants to get in your pants!"

Christine obviously wasn't happy about my latest remark. "Oh stop it! He's staying and that's final."

Before I could say another word, someone had rung our doorbell.

"Oh that's probably him." Christine said.

"What? He's here already?"

"Yes, Josh. Now play nice. Help me set up the table and try not to embarrass yourself tonight."

Christine walked away from the kitchen and headed to the front. Meanwhile I reluctantly set the table for the three of us.

I had always hated my boss, DeMarcus. We both worked in the accounting department of the local bank.

I had worked there since graduating from college. I practically had to beg to get my foot in the door there. Two years ago, my office manager let for a new company...and instead of promoting me, DeMarcus was hired to be my new boss!

I hated his guts. He stole my promotion! Worst of all, the guy bullied me non-stop. He was the typical "jock" from high school and he treated me like one of his nerd lackeys.

DeMarcus would often steal my pens at work, eat parts of my lunch, and play pranks on me in the office. Just the other day, he spiked my soda so it exploded all over my desk!

To everyone else, DeMarcus was charming and sweet...the perfect gentleman. He held the door for all the girls in the office. He surprised them with flowers.

For the other guys, he would surprise them with tickets to sought after sporting events and concerts. He even had HR in his pocket. I tried to complain to those guys a while ago, but they told me I must have been crazy because he was "such a

gentleman."

Ugh, it was only a week I guess. I just had to tough it out

for 7 days...

As I put down the last work on the table, my wife walked

back into the kitchen with a pair of booming footsteps not far

behind her.

It was DeMarcus. The guy was 6'5" so he basically towered

over my wife and I. His bald head shined under the light of the

ceiling.

Today he wore a pair of tight jeans and a t-shirt that

seemed one size too small. I guess that was on purpose though.

His black muscles flexed at every movement. He basically looked

like a Greek god.

"Josh! What's up homie!" DeMarcus ran up and gave me a bear

hug.

He really didn't know his own strength. His arms wrapped

around me and squeezed the air out of my chest. "Hey DeMarcus."

I grunted out.

"Hey thanks for letting me stay here." He said, patting me on the back.

"Uh yeah. Um...no problem." I said, trying to sound as genuine as I could.

"It's no problem," Christine said with a big smile on her face. "I hope you're hungry for chicken."

"Hungry? I'm starving!" DeMarcus proclaimed.

He sat down at on the table and began eating the chicken with his bare hands like a savage. Normally Christine and I ate with our forks and knives, but he didn't even use his.

"So," DeMarcus said with food still stuffed in his stupid mouth, "you guys mind if I have my side chick over tonight?"

"Oh go ahead, we don't mind." Christine chimed in before I could say anything. Why was she so accommodating to DeMarcus? I didn't want strangers over in our place.

"Great. Thanks Christine. I can always count on you." He said with a big smile.

Later that night Christine and I weren't really talking. I was a bit upset that she had invited DeMarcus over without consulting me.

In fact, we were just sitting there in bed together before we fell asleep without speaking a word to each other. I turned off the lights and drifted off to sleep.

It must have been about 1 AM or some ungodly hour of the night. I was woken up by the sounds of moaning. It must have been DeMarcus and his 'side chick'.

I heard the springs from the mattress in the other room bounce up and down. This poor woman's screams echoed throughout our house.

"Who owns your pussy you whore?"

"You do! DeMarcus!" She proclaimed.

"That's right you cunt! Bend over now. I'm going to tear

your pussy apart!"

"Hey, do you hear that?" I whispered to Christine as I glanced over at her.

It was a little dark, but I couldn't believe what I saw! Christine was playing with herself under the sheets while DeMarcus defiled that poor girl under our roof!

"Babe?" I said again, this time using a slightly louder voice.

"Shhhh! I can't hear."

"What?"

"I said 'shhhh', I'm trying to get some sleep."

I couldn't believe Christine was masturbating to DeMarcus fucking some random girl in our house.

I tried to go to bed, but I could only hear DeMarcus's booming voice every time I closed my eyes.

"Yeah suck on that cock you whore! You like it don't you?"

His voice could not have been more obnoxious. It took me a while to finally fall asleep that night.

Chapter 2

The next morning headed down to the kitchen to get my morning cup of coffee. I barely got four hours last night. DeMarcus was like a workhorse in the bedroom. He had sex with that girl for hours.

My head hurt from the lack of sleep. I picked up my first cup of coffee when DeMarcus waltzed right into the kitchen...actually he strutted in like he owned the place.

Christine smiled as she saw him come in. DeMarcus was only wearing his boxers. His six pack seemed to draw the attention of my wife.

"Sorry about the noise last night. I tried to shut her up." DeMarcus said with his deep voice.

I was about to tell him he kept us up all night, but Christine spoke first.

"Oh it was no problem. We really didn't hear much." She lied. I knew she was masturbating to the sound of their sex last night. It kind of bothered me, I had to admit.

I hadn't even drunk my first cup of coffee before DeMarcus jumped up off the chair with a piece of toast in his mouth.

"Hey Josh, we gotta bounce if we want to get into the office on time. I'll give you a lift."

"Aww, that's cute!" Christine said. "You two are going to work together in the same car!" She giggled.

Ugh, this day was already starting off bad.

We hopped in DeMarcus's black sports car and sped all the way to the office.

The rest of the week DeMarcus brought girl after girl after girl to our home.

It was like a non-stop orgy in our guest room. Every night he brought a new girl. Every night we heard him degrade those poor women.

And every night Christine seemed to become more and more turned on. I caught her masturbating to the noise the first night.

On the other nights, she went much further. Christine didn't even try to hide it anymore. She moaned along with whoever DeMarcus brought back home. I even thought she softly moaned his name one night.

The whole situation really bothered me. It wouldn't be much longer, though. DeMarcus's reign of terror would soon be over.

The next day I practically skipped to work. Everything seemed right again...well almost. All I had to do was get through one more night with DeMarcus.

I called my Christine later in the afternoon. "Hey babe, what are you doing?"

"I just woke up from a nap, are you still at work?"

"So listen. I know it's DeMarcus's last night here, but let's go out for a date tonight. Just the two of us. I missed it."

"Yeah I miss it too. Let's do it."

"Great, I'll see you at 6:00?"

"Sounds good."

I couldn't wait. I couldn't get off work fast enough.

As 5:30 approached, DeMarcus marched his way to my cubicle.

"Hey homie, what's up?" He said, all giddy for some reason. I could almost see my reflection against his pearly whites.

"Not much, about to head home," I said.

"Oh wait up, homie." DeMarcus said, holding up his enormous ape-like hand to stop me like a traffic man. "I need you to balance today's accounts before you leave today."

"What? Aren't the interns here to do that?"

Balancing the accounts in our book was a very tedious, but easy perform task. That's why we hired unpaid interns to do the work. I couldn't believe DeMarcus was making me do that!

"They're out sick. It shouldn't take you that long. I'll see you at home alright? I'll try to save you some chicken!"

DeMarcus smiled at me and patted me on the shoulder as he left...what a prick.

Great...I got stuck doing hours of work and missed out time to hang out with my wife. I was so angry I tried to get all the work done as fast as possible. I texted Christine the unfortunate news, but never heard back from her.

I didn't get done with the extra work DeMarcus dumped on me until 7:30. I raced home after that; maybe I could still do something with Christine.

As I pulled around the block, I saw Jamal's sports car already parked inside my garage. The nerve of that guy! He had the audacity to actually park in my garage after making me do extra work tonight.

I opened the door to the house with a hungry stomach. "Christine? Are you home?"

There was no answer.

"DeMarcus?"

No answer as well.

I heard a faint noise coming from our upstairs bedroom. I couldn't quite make out what it was so I decided to investigate.

As I approached the bedroom I could hear moans. It was Christine!...but there was someone else there as well.

"You're a tight little whore aren't you?"

"Mmmh! Oh god! I can't believe how big you are!"

"Who does your pussy belong to?!"

"You! It belongs to you! Please don't stop DeMarcus!"

Oh my god! It was DeMarcus fucking my wife!

Chapter 3

"Ohhhh yeaaah! Oh! Fuck me! Fuck fuck fuck! I love your big black cock!"

"Oh yeah, much bigger than Jason, right?"

"Oh he's a fucking pindick compared to you!"

I couldn't believe what I was hearing. DeMarcus was defiling my wife...in my own home...in my own bed!

Was this why he made me work late tonight? Had he fucked my wife before? I couldn't believe this was happening.

The door was left open. I peeked through the corner and saw the two of them.

Christine and DeMarcus were both naked. I saw his thick, black cock penetrate my wife's white little pussy.

I had never seen a cock that big. It must have been at least 11 inches. I had no idea how he was able to fit that thing inside my wife.

DeMarcus had bent my wife over the bed and fucked her over the edge. The sound of his balls slapping against her ass as he penetrated her filled my ears.

I stood there for a few moments completely in shock. Suddenly anger erupted from me like a volcano. I stomped my right foot forward.

"What the fuck?! What are you doing to my wife?"

DeMarcus looked back at me briefly before turning his attention back at my wife.

"Hey Jason. Finally finished those accounts? I'm just showing your wife how to have fun. She practically jumped on me when I told her you would be working late!"

He grabbed her hair from behind and pulled it roughly, jerking her head back and forth. Meanwhile, his cock pounded her from behind. Christine moaned with a mix of pain and pleasure.

I moved to the other side of the bed to look at my wife. Her eyes portrayed a mix of shock, excitement, and pleasure.

"Hey babe," she managed to say between her moans.

"What are you doing with him?" I pointed at the giant black man fucking my white wife.

"I couldn't resist him, babe." She admitted."

What in the world was I hearing?

"I loved hearing him fuck all those different girls every single night."

"They all do," DeMarcus said while chuckling.

"I just had to try him for myself. They sounded so satisfied. I just had to know...oh I just had to feel his big black cock in me."

There wasn't even a hint of shame in her voice.

"You wanted it that bad?"

"Oh! Yes. I wanted it so bad. Watch me, babe. Watch him

fuck me." She said with a calmness to her voice as her pussy was being destroyed by DeMarcus's big cock.

I didn't know what to do. I almost froze as too many thoughts raced in my head. For some reason I was turned on.

It was like watching live porn in my house. I know it was my wife, but I never made Christine moan and scream and beg like that. As I thought about it more and more, my cock began to stiffen in my pants.

Before I knew it, DeMarcus pulled his cock out of my wife's mouth. He grabbed her by the shoulders and lifted her onto her knees, facing him.

I moved to the other side of the bed so I could face Christine again.

DeMarcus stood at the edge of the bed and held his cock right against Christine's lips. He teased her by lightly taping is over-sized dick against her mouth, even slapping her a few times.

"Open your mouth, bitch!" He commanded her with a deep

voice.

Christine stretched out her mouth like she would at the dentist. She didn't even question his command.

DeMarcus grabbed the back of her head and jammed his black cock into her mouth.

He wasn't gentle at all. I was shocked by how hard he rammed it in. At the same time, my cock was straining against my pants. I continued to watch my wife be fucked with the utmost attention to detail.

"Are you okay?" I asked Christine.

"Mmm!" She said, as her voice was muffled my his cock.

DeMarcus shoved his cock down her mouth in one rapid motion after another. He grabbed the back of her head to get more leverage and increase the speed.

Meanwhile, she used his hand to slap her ass. The sound of skin on skin echoed through the entire house. I knew her ass was going to be red and sore in the morning.

Christine's moans were muffled by his cock.

"Oh yeah! Your wife has one TALENTED tongue!" DeMarcus remarked.

I found myself rubbing my dick through my pants as DeMarcus defiled my poor wife.

"Oh I'm going to cum soon." He announced. "Turn over, I want to cum in your dirty pussy!"

Christine scrambled to get on her back. DeMarcus climbed on the bed and mounted my wife in missionary.

I saw him jam his horse cock into my wife's sacred temple. Like always, he was not gentle at all.

"You want my cum don't you?"

"Oh yes! I want your warm cum in me! Please DeMarcus!"

"Ha ha. They all want my cum!" DeMarcus said while he glanced back at me.

"How bad do you want it?"

"Please, give me your cum!"

"Alright, you asked for it little bitch! Get ready!"

As DeMarcus picked up the pace of his thrusting, I finally noticed that he wasn't wearing a condom! He was fucking my wife with his bare cock! No protection at all!

My heart nearly jumped out of my chest. Christine and I had been trying to have a baby for the last month or so. This was exactly when she was the most fertile and she had this giant black guy fucking her.

I saw DeMarcus's muscles tighten. His legs spasmed. I knew this meant he was close to his orgasm.

"Oh YEEEEAAAH! Here it comes you cunt!" He announced at the top of his lungs.

I saw Christine's eyes light up when the first wave hit her. She screamed in pleasure as DeMarcus filled her up.

The guy had a giant pair of balls that were filled with cum. He was like a bull. He grunted as he kept thrusting into my wife.

"Oh! Oh god! Oh!" Christine bit down on her lip and rubbed her clit vigorously. She had reached her own orgasm after DeMarcus unloaded in her.

"Yeah you're a good whore, much better than all of the ones I've had before." DeMarcus claimed.

"Oh god, I've never experienced anything like that." Christine said softly.

I knelt down and held Christine's hand. Meanwhile, my cock was leaking in my pants after witnessing the hot sex that just happened in my own bed.

"Are you okay?" I asked her. It was a legitimate question...my wife had just been used by a big black bull as his fuck toy.

"I'm okay. Hey listen...I need you to go to the pharmacy. I

need you to get some Plan B."

"Yeah great idea," DeMarcus butted in. "I don't need any more whores asking me for alimony." He chuckled at his own remark.

"Okay." I said softly and kissed my wife on the forehead.

"Oh and don't forget to pick us up some Chinese." DeMarcus said as I left the room.

"Yeah, that would be great...we haven't eaten all night." Christine said with a smile on her face.

"Okay."

I left the room after I saw DeMarcus pull my wife on her knees and fucked her again.

I heard her moans as I left the house. I knew it was weird picking up dinner for DeMarcus and my wife, but I knew she wanted to fuck him more. Maybe after he was done I would be able to have her back. All I knew was I had to get that Plan B...

Hotwife Vacation

Jessie Sinclair

Copyright © 2017 Jessie Sinclair

All Rights Reserved

Chapter 1

"See anyone you like babe?"

"Come on Jake, do you really want to play this game again?"

"I do. What about him over there?"

I pointed across the bar where a handsome ebony man sat talking with his friends. Erin and I were sitting at the resort bar enjoying our vacation.

"Really? Come on, Jake."

"What?"

"He's not even that handsome. You want me to sleep with a man like that? I only want the good stuff like you."

Erin just laughed off my silly attempt to set her up with a ebony suitor.

"Well what about the other guy over there?"

"Babe, now you're just desperate to set me up." Erin said with a smile. She caressed my hand and circled down to my knee. A few moments later and her naughty hand began to stroke my cock to attention at the crowded bar.

"You're the only man I want to fuck." She said in a sultry voice.

Erin loved me and would never cheat, but sometimes I felt like she was bored with our sex life. And truth be told, I had a big fantasy of seeing her fucked by some gigantic black guy. I wanted him to tear her pussy up nice and hard for me.

We would often play this game on vacations, but Erin never really bit. It seemed like every guy I pointed towards wasn't good enough for her. This time was different, however. I was totally determined to see my ultimate fantasy come to fruition.

That's why I picked this resort. It was a completely nudist adult resort. I figured seeing a few big black dicks would really get her juices running...but no luck so far.

Erin drew a lot of attention from the locals for obvious reasons. She was a beautiful blonde goddess in this land of black. Her petite frame would certainly attract a few good suitors.

My wife wore a beautiful blue summer dress with a pair of sandals. Even I couldn't take my eyes off her busty rack.

"Come on, babe! Let's shop around."

"Hey, we're not buying a car or something. Sex is a very intimate thing. I'm just not comfortable with anyone here."

"Babe, we're on vacation in the middle of no where! It's totally okay to just have some fun."

Our waiter, Jamal, brought two more margaritas to our table.

"Here you are, it's on the house. Might I add...your wife is beautiful" He said with a big smile.

"Oh thank you very much." Erin replied.

Jamal began to step away, but quickly turned around. "If I may, I couldn't help but overhear your heated debate." He whispered to us.

It looked like blood left my wife's face. She turned a dark shade of red like a tomato.

"You know, we have a very hip club here at the resort. It's for a certain clientele if you understand what I'm saying."

I squinted at him. "What do you mean?"

"Well it attracts a lot of handsome local talent...you know black men who want white women. A lot of swingers like to go and have some fun with them. Everyone has a great time."

I couldn't believe what Jamal told us. It seemed like my dream.

"Where is it?" I asked.

"It's upstairs on the penthouse floor. Very secluded and secret. You'll have a ton of privacy."

There was no way I could turn down this opportunity. I caressed Erin's hand and pleaded with my eyes like a puppy dog.

"What do you say? Maybe we should just check it out?"

"Are you sure you want me to get fucked by some black strangers?"

"Of course! That's all I've been begging you for."

"Don't worry, the club is very safe. How about I put you down on the guest list." Jamal pressed further.

"See, babe? It'll be a ton of fun!"

"And tonight we have our glory hole night. You won't have to even see the other person if you don't want."

It was pretty much a sign from heaven at this point. "Well...I guess it couldn't hurt if we went for a little bit." Erin said in an unsure voice.

"Great! I'll make the arrangement and make sure you two are treated like a queen and king."

Jamal left without taking our check. I couldn't believe a

club like this actually existed. I sure did pick the perfect resort!

When Jamal was out of range, she whispered close to me. "Are you really sure you want to do this?"

"Of course! Why wouldn't I?"

"Well, I guess it would be a nice change of pace from your little pecker." She teased me.

"Alright it's settled! Let's go find you a big black cock!"

~~~Two hours later~~~

The night couldn't come fast enough. Erin and I had just finished getting ready for the big night. She wanted to dress up a little bit, but I insisted we keep it casual. If all went well, we wouldn't be wearing clothes for long anyways.

Erin wore a simple shirt with a pair of jeans. However, she still looked absolutely ravishing. Her hair flowed to the side as we walked together. We were both a little nervous, but I wanted to see this through.

As the elevator doors opened, we were greeted by a giant set of golden doors. The club didn't even have a name, but there were two guys in suits near the door.

"Hi, Jamal sent us. Our names are Jake and Erin."

The guy looked at his computer and quickly let us in. "Of course. Welcome and please enjoy yourself."

We walked into the club as smooth classical music played in the background. It looked like a large lounge with couches all over the place. Off in the distance, there were people shouting and cheering in another room.

It was certainly not what I had expected. "Whoa." I whispered softly to my wife. Off to the side, a few black men were taking some blonde woman as her husband watched and jerked off.

"Yeah, I'll say...there's a lot of good looking guys here." Erin said.

I smiled. I knew things would be getting pretty crazy

tonight.

Chapter 2

"Let's get a drink first." My wife said.

We pulled up at the bar and sat on the stools. The bartender quickly attended to our needs. "So, do you have any suggestions on how we should start out here?" I asked the man.

"Well, there's a glory hole wall in the next room." The guy said. "I suggest you start out there. You can sample many of the black cocks there and try it out for real if you like."

Wow I had no idea this place was so kinky. I had a hard time not getting hard imagining my wife slurping on some random guy's cock.

"Let's go." I said. I grabbed Erin's hand and led her into the room. It was pretty crazy. We stood in the center of a circular room. Every two feet there was a big black cock sticking out of the wall. A few other couples were already playing with the toys, and I was eager to get started.

"Wow they're so beautiful..." Erin marveled at the cocks. "I want one right now!"

She knelt down to the far left section of the wall. She grabbed it with her hand it was so big compared to her pale white fingers. "It's go big!" She whispered to me.

"You've never had black cock before have you?" The man from the other side of the wall said.

"Never." Erin replied.

"Go on...suck on it. I know you want to."

Erin looked back at me and I encouraged her to go on. My cock was rock hard at this point.

My wife bent down and placed her lips on the head. She kissed it before moving in and sucking on it. "Oh!" Erin moaned. She just had her first taste of black cock. She really started deep throating all 10 inches of this massive cock.

"Ugh! Yes! Keep going!" The man ordered my wife in a deep, confident voice. "You're going to be a good slut for me!"

Erin began caressing this man's balls and stroked his

shaft. "We've got a really good cock sucker here!" He announced to the others.

"How many of you are back there?" I asked.

"Two." He replied.

"I'll come out and meet you."

Meanwhile, another man took his place and stuck his big cock through the slit. He was even larger at 12 inches. My wife could hardly contain her excitement at this point. She sucked on that thing like a wild whore. I'm pretty sure everyone could hear Erin's moans at this point.

Before long a tall, dark, and handsome guy walked through the door completely naked. He towered five inches over me and was built like a linebacker.

"Hello, you must be the cock sucker's cuck." He said with a smile. "I'm Marko."

"Hi." I said, somewhat intimidated by his large stature.

He pulled up my wife while his friend shouted back. "Hey! She was sucking on my cock, Marko! I've never had anything so good before!"

"Calm down, Tony. I'm just meeting this beautiful woman. And believe me, she's hot!"

"Hello, I'm Marko." He said, grabbing my wife's hand and kissing it like a gentleman.

"Wow, you're so handsome. I-I'm Erin."

"And what's a beautiful goddess like you doing in such a place?"

"She wants black cock." I answered for her as we all laughed.

"Well you've come to the right place."

"Your cock is so amazing." Erin said almost in complete disbelief.

"I know. That's what they all say." He replied.

"Hey, my cock is getting soft over here!" Tony shouted through the wall.

Erin laughed. "Don't worry. I'm coming. I'll make it all better." She knelt down again and sucked on his balls. They were the size of large golf balls. My wife popped them in and massaged them with her tongue. She stroked the top of his black cock before moving her lips up.

"Oh yeah! I knew you were a good cock sucker!" Tony shouted.

Meanwhile, Marko moved down and stripped my wife naked. He didn't even ask for permission! He grabbed her breast and examined it. "Dang Tony! This slut has some big ass tits!"

"Really?"

"You like?"

"Of course I do." Marko moved over and sucked on her nipples while she moaned. Her hand still stroked Tony's cock through the glory hole. I couldn't believe what was happening!

"Dang! You should see her pussy!" Marko moved in and inserted his finger into my wife as she moaned.

"Oh god!" Erin bit down on her lip. His large finger was pretty much the size of my cock.

"Hold on! I'm coming!" Tony announced.

I head a rush of footsteps like a stampede as Tony ran into the room. He was built like his companion. Tony had broad shoulders, a big chest, and an incredible smile. I knew my wife would love to be taken by every inch of his cock.

"Wow she's much hotter than I imagined." Tony remarked. He watched as his friend pleasured my wife with his fingers. Erin leaned in and kissed Marko on the lips. Her moans became noticeably louder; my cock stiffened in response.

"Oh take me! I want you boys to take me!" She moaned.

"Here?" I asked.

"No let's do it in the lounge. We haven't had a good show

in a while. I'm sure everyone will be excited."

My wife getting fucked in the lounge? It was a little more public in my fantasies, but I saw the look on Erin's face. She wanted it bad and I couldn't resist her eyes. She was addicted to black cock now and she wanted to be ravaged!

"Sure, let's go." My wife said.

Erin walked with a black bull on each arm as I scurried along like an obedient cuck. My cock twitched at the thought of my wife being taken like this.

Chapter 3

Tony held my wife's hand and guided her to an open table with a couch. Erin couldn't keep her eyes off their massive black cocks. It seemed like the boys had her in an erotic trace. Tony was very hands on with her. His dark paws groped my wife's breasts.

He smiled as he his fingers pinched her nipples. He began to suck on them as she moaned softly. Marko went in and sucked on the other one. Erin moaned and looked at me with a devious smile as the black boys feasted on her bounty.

Erin gripped both of their cocks and slowly jerked them off. "Oh they're so big, honey! They're so much bigger than you!"

My cock grew harder by the second. I took off my pants and began to jerk off. A little bit of pre-cum even dripped from the tip.

Just then, Tony's placed his fingers between Erin's legs. His fucked my wife with them. She moaned into Marko's mouth as they embraced for a passionate kiss. The sounds of their faces sucking on each other drove me insane.

I knelt down before the touch and rubbed her smooth legs. She spread them wide as Tony banged her pussy. "Oh! Yes! Oh god!" She moaned.

I could see her body convulse and her muscles tighten as she succumbed to a powerful orgasm. When Tony pulled out his fingers, they were covered with Erin's white gloss. He smelled it and took a little taste. "Mmm you taste good."

He rubbed his fingers all over my wife's lips. "Taste yourself." He command.

I looked around and a few people were beginning to stare at us. I didn't care at this point; I was just having fun and it made the entire situation so much more naughty!

"How does it feel?" I asked her.

"I want their cocks so bad!"

"Yeah? You do?"

"Of course I do!"

"Are you ready for us?!" Both bulls stood triumphantly with their rods hanging proudly in sight.

"I've never wanted anything more." My wife said. She arched her head back and rubbed her clit as Marko rammed his cock into her tiny pussy.

Tony grabbed my wife's head as she knelt on the couch. "I bet you want to suck my cock!"

"Yes! Please! I want it!" Erin begged him like a whore. My cock twitched in response.

"Suck on it, slut!"

Erin wrapped her lips around Tony's head; they barely wrapped around his monster cock. She began choking hard on his 12 incher. I jerked off in response.

"How good does it taste babe?"

"So amazing! Yours never tasted so good!" She sighed.

I watched as Marco's hands caressed my wife's hips. Her whole body tingled with pleasure as he ran over the length of her smooth and silky legs. He grabbed her ass tightly and slapped it a few times.

By this time, everyone had focused their attention on us. We were the main event!

Marko's dick rammed into my wife from behind. He fucked her like a dog. I moved closer to watch his big black cock tear her pussy apart. It stretched so far to accommodate something so big. I knew that her pussy would never wrap around my cock the same way again.

"God! It hurts!" She whispered to me.

I held her hand tightly. "You can do this babe. I believe in you." Erin nodded as her slutty mouth continued to pleasure Tony.

Marko grabbed Erin's waist and rammed his cock harder and faster. His balls flew around everywhere like a pinball machine. Her pussy juices dripped down the back of her legs. Marko pumped deeper and deeper into my wife. It seemed like his cock only grew harder by the minute.

"God! Your cunt is tight as fuck!"

Erin's hips gyrated from side to side. However, her screams were muffled by Tony's big cock. He grabbed the back of her head and really jammed his cock down her throat. I loved to listen to her gag on it.

I moved in closer to see the action up close. All of a sudden, Erin grabbed my dick and jerked me off! Her strokes coordinated with the punishment she took. I moaned softly and arched my head back. Her silky finger tips guided me to heaven.

Marko tore my wife's pussy apart. I watched his big black cock stretch out her tiny, dirty cunt. Every stroke of his cock seemed like an eternity. Erin shuddered in a complete ecstasy; it looked like she was possessed by the devil.

"Cum in me boys. I want you to fill up my holes!" She begged.

"Hear that Marko?"

"Yeah, the whore wants our cum!"

"Let's do it!"

"Are you ready for our cum!"

"Yes!" Erin pleaded with them.

The big black boys began to pump faster into my wife. They stood at opposite sides and destroyed her pussy and mouth. She screamed like a banshee as more and more men surrounded us to jerk off in a circle. They wanted to see the entertainment up close.

Erin had developed a killer grip on my cock as she jerked it around randomly. I tried my best to hold it all in, but I passed the point of no return.

"Cum in her! Please! Cum in her holes!" I begged them. I let loose and came all over Erin's lower back. My white seed continued to pour out as I panted like a dog.

My wife begged the boys some more as they let loose as

well. Marko's balls swelled up as he completely unloaded in her. Tony exploded in her mouth. When Marko pulled out, his cum gushed onto the floor.

Tony rubbed his cock all over Erin's lips. They were covered with his cum.

I looked down and Erin's pussy looked so swollen and beat up. She was going to be sore for days on end. I looked around and the other black guys at the club smiled at us.

"Circle jerk! Circle jerk!" They chanted loudly.

Marko, Tony, and I moved aside at the rest of them lined up to unload on my wife. I saw wave after wave of black cum shoot all over my wife's body. By the time they were done, she was absolutely drenched with it all.

I held her closely in my arms. The cum was still warm. "Are you okay?"

"I'm okay." She whispered and nodded.

"That was so hot!"

"I know."

Erin and I kissed. I tasted a bitter sweet sensation on my
tongue...it was the taste of black cock and knowing my wife had
been deflowered!

Taken At The Pool

Jessie Sinclair

Copyright © 2017 Jessie Sinclair

All Rights Reserved

Chapter 1

"Hey babe, should I wear this pair of black swim trunks or the red one?" I asked my wife Sarah as I looked at the mirror.

"Whatever you want." She said coldly.

"Well what are you wearing?" I made my way into the bathroom where my wife was putting on her makeup.

Why she would need makeup for a pool party was beyond me. I mean wasn't it going to wash off in the water anyways? Seemed like a waste of time.

Sarah sighed noticeably. "I'm going to wear this bikini."

Wow Sarah looked incredible. She was wearing a pink little bikini. It looked one size too small. The thing barely covered her ass and almost left her nipples visible.

"What? You're wearing that?"

"Yes, Tim. I'm going to wear this bikini." She flashed me a somewhat annoyed glare from the mirror. "You're not going to be a party-pooper and embarrass me in front of my friends at work are you?"

"Of course I won't! Do you not want me there?" I asked, somewhat dejected.

"Well I just don't think this type of party is your scene." She said with a sincere voice.

She did have a good point. I worked in the finance world. We wore suits to work and everything was formalized. Meanwhile, Sarah worked in the marketing arm at some hot new tech startup.

Sarah and her colleagues had a laid back culture. They wore shorts and flip flops to work. They played pool and ping pong and drank beer during office hours. The culture was completely different from what I was used to.

Plus it didn't help that I was in my late thirties while Sarah was in her mid twenties.

We met through work. My firm had helped hers secure a bank loan. I happened to run into Sarah in the lobby one day at their office and we really hit it off. We got married shortly after our whirlwind romance.

It always bothered me that Sarah would dress in very short skirts and revealing tops to go to work even after we married. I never said anything because I didn't want to upset her. Plus, she was kind of out of my league as well.

Well, it looked like today would be no different judging by her skimpy bikini.

"What? You don't think I'll be able to hang with you and your colleagues?"

"Well no...just wanted to make sure you wanted to come."

"I do, are you almost ready?"

"Yeah let's go."

Earlier this week Sarah had surprised me by inviting me to her office pool party. Her boss, Jamal was hosting it at his house.

Historically, Sarah never invited me to her office parties

or even dinner events for some reason. I pleased and begged her to let me come for the past year and she finally gave in I guess.

This was one opportunity I wouldn't want to miss out on. I always wanted to see her in action at work.

We hopped in the car. I followed Sarah's directions and we were at Jamal's in less than half an hour. We pulled up to a gigantic mansion on a cliff. It looked like something out of a Hollywood movie.

"Wow...this place is amazing." My jaw practically fell to the floor.

"It's Jamal's place." Sarah said nonchalantly.

"Really?"

"Yep."

I knew things were going good at her work, but I never imagined things were THAT good.

All of a sudden I felt quite poor pulling up to the driveway in my Toyota sedan. I took a quick look around and there were half dozen expensive sports cars littered along the garage.

Standing by the front door was a well-built black man in his early twenties. He looked like he jumped out of an Abercrombie magazine.

He wore nothing except for a pair of short swimming trunks. His body was to die for. Even I was jealous.

His arms were bigger than my legs. Each muscle seemed to glisten under the sun. His six pack seemed to scream 'stare at me!'

We left the car and this handsome man looked in our direction.

"Sarah! Glad you made it...and on time as well!"

Sarah's face lit up. "Hey Charlie!"

Sarah walked up and kissed him on both cheeks. Charlie

towered over her, so he had to naturally bend down a little. The guy must have been at least 6'4".

"So Charlie, this is my husband Tim."

"Hi Tim, I'm Charlie. Sarah and I work together." His bright white teeth almost blinded me.

I shook his hand and felt his monster grip.

"Hi." I said trying not to show signs of weakness after experiencing Charlie's vice grip.

"Welcome, the party is out in the backyard." He turned over and looked at Sarah for a second. "I think Jamal was looking for you."

"Oh okay." She said, almost blushing.

I wondered what that was all about.

"Well it was nice meeting you, Charlie. I think we're going to join the party now."

"Have fun." He said as we walked away.

We walked into the back and it was quite the scene. Jamal sure did have a nice place.

There were probably about 20 - 30 people in his Olympic-sized infinity pool. Off to the side were three or four Jacuzzis that could each sit five or six people.

Everyone there seemed to be scantily dressed. The guys only wore shorts and the girls wore skimpy bikinis. In fact, there were quite the few naked party-goers running around.

Suddenly, I felt horribly out of place. Everyone here seemed to work out a lot and looked like the Greek Gods and Goddesses.

I mean I didn't look out of shape, but these twenty year-olds put me to shame with their well-built bodies.

I was beginning to wonder what I had gotten myself into.

Chapter 2

"Hey, you didn't tell me there would be naked people at the party!" I whispered into Sarah's ear.

"Well I told you it wasn't your scene. We can still go if you want." She replied.

"No, its okay, I'll just stick around. I can handle it."

"Alright, just go make yourself a drink. I'm going to try and find Jamal."

I headed back into the kitchen where every type of alcohol and beer could be found. I looked around and decided to make myself a Vodka Soda.

Before long, some big breasted blonde in a tiny bikini came strutting into the kitchen.

"I haven't seen you around here. I'm Jessica, who are you?"

I was absolutely floored by this beautiful girl. The name Jessica rang a bell. I think I remembered Sarah talking about her once or twice.

Apparently Jessica was some kind of promiscuous girl at the office. She certainly seemed like it the way she was dressed. I didn't really care though; I could hardly keep my eye off her boobs.

"H-Hi! I-I'm uh Tim. I'm Sarah's husband."

"Sarah's husband?"

"Yeah...she did tell you about me, right?"

"Oh right, sorry! Typical dumb blonde had one too many drinks, right?" She said while pointing at her head.

I thought it was weird that Sarah had never mentioned me to her co-workers. I chugged my drink and decided to get another one.

"Hey, what do you say we do a shot?" Jessica said as she grabbed the collar of my shirt with her finger seductively. I could smell the alcohol on her breath.

"I-isn't it a little early for shots?" I said. I didn't want to wake up the next morning with a big hangover.

"Oh come on!"

"Ummm..."

"I guess Sarah was right about you." She said while pouting.

"What? What did she say about me?"

Jessica hesitated for a second. She seemed afraid about talking too much. "Well, she said you're kind of a party-pooper."

"What?" That's crazy! You want to do a shot? Let's do one then!"

"Great!" Jessica said with a smile. This young, busty twenty-year old blonde had just tricked me into doing a shot with her.

"Hmmm." Jessica said as she surveyed our choices. She

grabbed a clear bottle of tequila.

"Let's do a shot of tequila."

She poured us two giant shots. I couldn't believe I was about to do this.

"Alright Tim, bottoms up!"

I downed the shot in one gulp. My worst fears were realized when I felt the liquor slowly slide down my throat. It was a slight burning sensation. I almost threw up.

"Oh god!" I choked as I finished the shot.

"How was it?" Jessica laughed.

I was about to respond when I glanced out the window. It appeared to be my wife, Sarah, kissing that guy Charlie from earlier! I couldn't have been right. They were making out right by the pool.

"Hey is that Sarah making out with Charlie?" I asked Jessica.

"Oh I don't know. Probably not." She said calmly while pouring herself another drink.

I know I already had two drinks, but I knew what I saw. I decided to head straight for the pool to confront her about this.

I headed out towards the side leaving Jessica behind. There were a ton of people in my way and loud music blasting from the DJ booth not too far away.

I waddled around like a duck until I got to the pool. Sarah wasn't kissing Charlie anymore. Instead, she was talking to another black man.

This black guy must have been nearly seven feet tall. He was even larger and muscular than Charlie. It seemed like he was flexing his gigantic muscles to tease Sarah.

Sarah was hooked. She wrapped her arms around his large biceps and squeezed.

I walked up to them. "Hey Sarah, can I talk to you for a

second?"

"Tim! Where did you go? I've been looking for you. I want you to meet someone!" I could tell Sarah had been drinking a little as she slurred a few of her words.

The man turned at me and smiled. His chiseled jaw opened to reveal his pearly whites. His smile could make any girl weak to her knees. This man was incredibly handsome; even I had to admit that.

"Hi, I'm Jamal. Sarah and I work together."

Wow so this was her boss? I couldn't believe she worked with such a hunk. I was jealous she spent so much time with this god.

"Uh h-hi, I'm Tim. I'm her husband." I had to look up to make eye contact with Jamal. He absolutely towered over me.

We shook and my hands looked like a little baby compared to his. It seemed like his grip could easily crush coconuts.

"So are you enjoying my party?" He said with a smile.

"Uh yeah, everything is fun. Thanks for inviting us."

I grabbed Sarah's hand. "Hey, can I talk to you about something?"

Jamal interrupted me. "Hey Tim, where's your drink? We have a rule here, everyone needs to have a drink by the pool!"

He lightly pushed me backwards in a joking manner, however he didn't even know his own strength and I was thrown back a few steps.

He turned to the side table and picked up a bottle of beer. "Here, take this." He handed me his beer.

I took his drink, not daring to say no to this man.

Jamal then turned to Sarah. "Hey babe, you want to go in the pool?"

"I thought you'd never ask!" She said while blushing.

I could tell her nipples were hard under her bikini. Was

she really that turned on by her big black boss?

Sarah looked in my direction. "You want to join us?" She said.

I really couldn't swim well, so I declined.

"Oh come on! Don't be such a wuss!" Jamal teased me.

"Oh it's okay. You two go ahead. I'm going to just chill out here."

"Okay, suit yourself." She said.

Before I could say anything Jamal grabbed Sarah by the waist and tossed her into the pool. "Oh my god!" Sarah cried out in laughter. Jamal jumped in after that. A big splash hit the other party people as they cheered.

The party goers began to cheer. "Kiss! Kiss! Kiss!"

Why were they doing that?

Sarah looked at me briefly before turning back at Jamal,

who was right across from her.

I stared at Sarah as she made eye contact with Jamal and smiled. I couldn't believe what I was seeing. I was so stunned I couldn't even utter any words to stop this madness.

"Kiss! Kiss! Kiss!" I heard the crowd continue to chant.

Sarah jumped up and Jamal caught her against his chest. The two locked lips in a passionate love making session.

Oh god, I thought I was going to be sick to my stomach. I didn't think the parties got this wild. How could she do that to me?

I was going to jump in the pool and say something, but Jessica stepped in front of me.

"Hey you! You slipped away from me a while ago. Enjoying the party?"

Chapter 3

Oh great. It was Jessica. She was the last person I wanted to talk to right now.

"Uh no not really." I tried to walk to the side, but she blocked my way.

"Hey where do you think you're going?"

"Jessica, look now is not the time. I just saw my wife make out with Jamal. I've got to do something."

Jessica looked at me for a moment, collecting her thoughts. She laughed a little to my surprise.

"Oh stop it. Don't worry, Tim. Everyone at work fucks each other all the time...sometimes even at the office. It's nothing to worry about."

"Nothing to worry about? Are you crazy?"

I pushed Jessica off to the side as I tried to find Sarah and Jamal again. They were nowhere to be found in the pool.

Where did they disappear off to? They were like a pair of magicians.

"Hey, where did they go?"

"If you must know, they're probably in Jamal's bedroom upstairs." She said calmly, while taking another sip of her drink.

"Alright, thanks. I'll be right back."

"Don't be gone for too long!" Jessica teased me with a sultry voice as she playfully slapped my cheeks.

I sprinted back into the house into the living room. The floor was lined with an exquisite marble that must have cost thousands. I ran up the ornate white spiral staircase to the second floor.

Eventually I found the master bedroom. As I approached, I heard a woman moaning. I gulped as I realized my worst fears.

I tiptoed into the room and saw Sarah kneeling on the king-sized bed. From behind, Jamal was fucking her pussy. Meanwhile,

Charlie was standing at the edge of the bed, thrusting his cock into my wife's throat.

"Ohhhh!" Sarah moaned into Charlie's cock.

I couldn't believe these two large, built black guys were double teaming my wife!

Charlie pulled his cock out of her mouth for a moment and slapped it on her lips. Sarah graciously licked it like a lollipop.

"What are you guys doing?" I said. My voice clearly sounded distraught.

"Oh hey, Tim!" Jamal said with a hearty attitude. Charlie managed to say hi in between his moans as Sarah sucked his cock. She pulled it out of her mouth and an audible pop could be heard.

"Hey babe." She said calmly. She wasn't even embarrassed that I caught her fucking these two studs.

I was stunned. I was petrified. Was my wife really fucking

these two large black stallions?

"What are you doing?" I asked Sarah again.

"Just having fun babe. I told you...our work parties weren't your scene." Her voice was emphatic.

Boy...she wasn't kidding. While I was stunned at this revelation, I was oddly turned on. The sight of two big black cocks taking advantage of my white wife seemed oddly hot.

"Here, sit and watch." Jamal commanded with his deep, booming voice. Jamal towered over me like I was some kind of midget. I didn't dare get on his bad side. He could have easily flicked me across the room with one hand.

I sat down on the small sofa in front of the bed and watched the events unfold.

"Hey, what are you doing? Suck my cock you little white whore!" Charlie commanded my wife like she was some common prostitute. He slapped her face with his dick for emphasis.

Sarah got the hint and began sucking on his cock again. She

focused her lips and tongue on his large head, before trying to

swallow his big black cock. It must have been at least nine

inches long. I couldn't believe she could fit that in her mouth.

Charlie grabbed the back of her head and fucked his cock

down her throat with no regard to her gagging. I was going to

say something, but Jamal began to insert his black cock into my

wife's pussy.

Jamal was even more impressive than Charlie. His cock was

over 11 inches long! It certainly put my four inch cock to

shame.

Jamal inserted his cock slowly at first. I saw Sarah's eyes

widen as she realized what was happening. The pain of his large

cock must have been indescribable.

Sarah moaned into Charlie's cock as Jamal finally inserted

his entire cock into her tight little pussy. He grabbed her at

the waist and began fucking her in doggy. Every thrust forward

pushed her forward into Charlie's cock.

"Oh!! Mmmm!" Sarah moaned as these two big black studs

violated her body. I did nothing but watch. My cock was almost hard and dripping wet at the scene.

Charlie and Jamal ignored me for the most part. They were more focused on getting their rocks off.

"Wow Jamal, can you believe how good our little white whore sucks cock?"

"Yeah man! She wants our black dicks so bad!"

Charlie pulled his cock out of her mouth and placed it on her chin. "Do you want my cum, little whore?"

Sarah looked at me for a second. I nodded my head slightly, showing my reluctant approval.

She turned back to face his cock. "Yes Charlie, I want your cum!"

"Beg for my cum, you little white whore! Beg me like a good slut!"

"Please may I have your cum!"

"Shut up and get sucking then!" He forcibly jammed his cock
into her lips.

"Gah!" Sarah gagged as Charlie's cock fucked her throat.
Meanwhile, Jamal fully inserted his cock into her pussy and
stopped trusting. He bent forward and watched the firework
spectacle in progress.

"Oh you white whore! You want my black cum don't you!"

"Mm hm!" Sarah grunted as she took his cock deeper and
deeper.

"I'm going to cum in your mouth!"

I watched with high anticipation. I was nearly on the edge
of the couch at this point.

Charlie's body tightened and he spasmed as my wife's tongue
brought him over the edge. Charlie began erupting in her mouth.

Sarah began choking on his cum. After a few seconds,
Charlie pulled his cock out. He was still cumming. He angled his
cock up and sprayed Sarah's eyes...and well her entire face

really.

After a few seconds, his orgasm finally died down. I could barely recognize my wife with so much cum on her face. The white liquid was all over and dripped from her mouth.

"Wow..." Jamal commented. "How long were you holding that one in?" He laughed.

"Oh about a week man. You have no idea. I wanted to drench this white whore with my cum. Now lick it all up." Charlie said with a little bit of hubris in his voice.

He picked up his clothes from the floor and left the room. "Had fun with you Sarah. Let's do this again at the next party."

He said as he walked out. Charlie didn't even acknowledge my presence after he came all over my wife's face.

I knelt down in front of Sarah and watched the cum drip off her face. She wiped it off with her hand and looked at me in the eyes. It was the first time we had made real eye contact since I caught her in the act.

"Alright, you ready for my cum too, you whore?"

Sarah looked at me without saying anything. "It's okay." I told her softly.

"Yes Jamal. I want your cum!"

"Get ready for it then you white slut!"

Jamal lifted her pussy up and jammed his cock in there with full force.

Sarah's eyes rolled up to the back of her head as she moaned. It sounded like a mix of pain and pleasure. Jamal began pumping his cock into her pussy.

He was moving so fast and hard I was afraid he would break something. "Oh god, your pussy is so tight you whore! I'm going to STRETCH it out!"

"Oh god! It hurts! Oh god! It feels so good!" Sarah grunted and screamed. Her voice was becoming more and more high pitched.

"Oh here it comes! Are you ready?"

"Yes! I want your black cum! Please!"

"Here it is, whore!"

Jamal gave it one more hard thrust and he came inside her pussy. It was at that moment I realized he wasn't wearing a condom!

My wife's big black boss was fucking her with no protection! After a few seconds Jamal pulled out and all his cum leaked out of her pussy. It must have been a giant load.

Jamal walked towards Sarah's face and pushed me to the side. "Here, lick my cum off my dick."

Sarah graciously accepted his offering and licked it all off like a ice cream cone.

"That's my white whore!" Jamal grabbed her by the hair and lifted her head up. "Thanks for the fun babe. Let's do this again next time."

Sarah nodded. "Yes, I'd love that." She said in a very

submissive voice.

"Good." He said while chuckling. "See you back at the pool later. Hope you had fun, Tim!" He said, while leaving the room.

Sarah stayed on the bed while I held her hands. All of her holes had been fucked by those two black studs. She was covered with their cum.

I was mad at her earlier, but now I was just turned on.

"Are you okay babe?"

"Yeah, I'm fine. Just a bit tired and sore. Why don't we go home?"

"Home? We still have a party here!" I said with a smile on my face.

Sarah laughed. "Okay let's go get drinks."

As we walked down the stairs Sarah looked at me and smiled. "So did you enjoy the show?"

"I loved it." I said, pointing to the wet spot in my

shorts. Let's do another one soon."

Sarah laughed at me. "Sure thing babe."

We both headed back to the party for more fun...

Taken In The Bahamas

Jessie Sinclair

Copyright © 2017 Jessie Sinclair

All Rights Reserved

Chapter 1

Jessica and I stepped out of our limo ride from the airport. We were staying at the Atlantis in the Bahamas for our honeymoon. We had married hours back in the states.

The humid air of this beautiful tropical island swarmed around my skin like a warm blanked. Beads of sweat formed on the top of my head.

I stepped out of the car to help Jessica with her step. I gently held her hand and lifted her out of the limo. We thanked the driver with a small tip before he left.

The majestic resort stood in front of us. Fountains, statues, and water parks highlighted the many amenities of this incredible destination.

"Wow, this place looks beautiful." Jessica gasped as she surveyed our home for the next week.

"Yeah, I'll say! So, ready to start our honeymoon off with a bang Mrs. Johnson?" I extended my arm out for Jessica as I escorted her into the resort. A bell boy followed behind with our luggage.

We checked in at the front desk Lisa the receptionist.

"Okay Mr. And Ms. Jake Johnson, you are all checked in. I'm having DeAndre give you a tour of our facilities. It's a big place so it's easy to get lost. Here's a map and I've circled your room number here. You can also download it on your phone to get detailed directions in case you get lost."

"Great, thank you." I replied with delight.

Lisa phoned DeAndre on the phone who came running over a few minutes later. Wow, even I had to admit he was the definition of an alpha male.

DeAndre towered over Jessica and me. He must have been at least 6'4". His bold muscles seemed to flex with every movement. DeAndre was shirtless, only wearing a pair of tight board shorts and flip flops.

I could tell with the bulge in his pants that he was packing some real heat. Jessica noticed as well. I saw that she was checking out his junk. It didn't matter to me. Even I had to admit he was a real man's man.

He finally reached us. "Hi, I'm DeAndre!"

I shook hands with this man who could have rivaled the
Greek gods. "Hi DeAndre, I'm Jake."

We shook hands and let me tell you this guy had a killer
grip. I'd had to be on the wrong end of a choke-hold with this
guy!

"This is my wife Jessica."

"Jessica! What a beautiful name!" DeAndre shook hands with
my wife. His black hand was in stark contrast with my wife's
pale white skin.

DeAndre brought her hands to his lips and kissed. "Wow what
a beautiful bride you have."

She giggled at DeAndre's attempts to flirt with her.

"So are you newlyweds ready for a tour of our beautiful
resort?"

"Yep, we can't wait to take a look around."

"Okay! Follow me to our majestic ride."

DeAndre's 'majestic ride' turned out to be a high end golf cart.

"Come Mrs. Johnson; let's get you on my sweet ride." DeAndre carefully held Jessica's hand to ease her onto the front seat.

I thought DeAndre was being a little too flirty, but I didn't care too much. At the end of the night, it would be me who would be taking Jessica back to our bedroom for some fun.

DeAndre showed me the back seat of the cart. His muscles glistened against the shine of the sun. I was a bit jealous of his ripped body, but that was part of the job. He needed to look good for the wealthy hotel patrons.

"So, I'm going to take you to see the hotel bar first." DeAndre explained. "You, Mr. Johnson, seem like a guy who can hold his liquor." He teased me.

I had to admit, DeAndre was a guy who could make you feel like a million bucks.

"Oh me? Haha. Well I guess I've had my fair share."

"Oh don't be coy!" Jessica jumped into the conversation. She practically burst out laughing. "Jake here can drink almost anyone to shame!"

"Oh really? Then you'll love our hotel bar." DeAndre explained. "We have over 30 types of rum."

"Really? That's incredible!"

"Yes, it is. You have to sample our hotel brand. It's brewed locally here."

I was savoring the opportunity to try the rum later.

DeAndre spent the next half hour giving us the complete tour of the resort. He showed us the best lunch/dinner restaurants, the hottest beach spots, and even gave us tips on avoiding the long lines at the water park.

Throughout the tour, I couldn't help but notice how Jessica was checking him out. I mean I guess I couldn't help it as well. His body was just so well built. He even flirted with both of us. It was part of the island charm I guess.

DeAndre dropped us off back at our room. It was on the seventh floor of the main tower of the resort. "OK Mr. and Ms. Johnson, here is your hotel!" He extended his hand out to present our humble abode for the next week.

Jessica and I made barely made it into hour room before she pushed me against the wall and kissed me passionately. Her hands followed down to my pants as she unzipped it with a flurry. Before I knew it, we were both naked and she was devouring my cock with a passion I had not yet seen.

She was wild and horny and begging me to fuck her senseless.

"Come on Jake. Fuck me hard. I'm so horny. I want cock so bad!" She exclaimed.

I was so turned on by her aggressiveness that I didn't last

more than a few minutes. I came too quickly.

Jessica closed her eyes when I entered her. By her the feel of her glistening wet pussy, I suspected she was fantasizing about DeAndre's big black cock stretching her out.

That thought sent me over the edge as I spurt my load into her. I pushed my cock deeper into her pussy as my hot cum shot out.

Jessica held me close as we kissed. No words were exchanged between us, just pure animal pleasure. This honeymoon was off to a good start.

Chapter 2

The next morning I awoke to Jessica getting dressed in front of the bathroom mirror.

Apparently she had gone out to breakfast while I slept like a baby. She had flirted with DeAndre again, which made her extra horny.

She took care of my morning wood with her talented mouth and tongue pretty quickly.

"So, Jake, I want to go to the beach today. DeAndre told me about this really romantic spot near this amazing cliff. He said the views at sunset are incredible."

"Well, I guess we have to check it out then."

Jessica finished putting on her makeup and slipped into a sexy pink and turquoise bikini. The tight silky fabric barely covered her beautiful breasts and ass cheeks.

I myself slipped into swimming shorts and put on my flip flops.

Jessica and I headed out to the beach. It was pretty secluded; only a few other couples were around.

The warm sand crumbled between our toes. The sun's blaze against our skin. The ocean water was nearly transparent. Our view couldn't have been more beautiful.

We set up a tent near the water. Before long, Jessica and I couldn't take our hands off each other. We kissed under the tent.

"So, do you want to do something crazy?" She whispered to me.

"Like what?"

"Well, I was thinking we get fucked up on that rum and have sex on the beach."

My eyes lit up. I liked the sound of her idea, but I was afraid someone would catch us in the act.

"That sounds good, but what if someone catches us?"

"Oh come on, don't be such a schoolboy, Jake. We're on our honeymoon; we'll only get to do this once."

What she said made sense. "Well okay, I guess we could do it. But where would we even get the rum?"

"DeAndre told me he was working lifeguard duty today. He said he'd be in a tower a quarter of a mile from where we are."

"Okay, let's go check it out I guess."

Jessica and I hiked the short distance to the lifeguard tower overlooking this portion of the beach. It didn't look like anyone was inside.

I climbed up first and knocked on the door before opening it. "Hey DeAndre? Are you working here?"

There was no answer. We walked in and the placed smelled like some hardcore weed. "Wow do you smell that?"

"Yeah I guess DeAndre has a thing for weed." Jessica giggled.

The toilet inside flushed and we hear the running water from a faucet. A few moments later DeAndre surfaced from the bathroom near the back of the room.

His eyes lit up when he saw Jessica. "Well if it isn't my favorite couple!" He announced.

"Hi DeAndre." Jessica said with a big smile. I could see she was checking him out. DeAndre was wearing just a pair of tight shorts like the last time we saw him.

"So what brings you two here."

"Well we were thinking about trying some of that rum you were talking about before. We wanted to get fucked up on it."

DeAndre chuckled to himself. "Oh I'm sure you do! I knew I liked you when I first met you."

He went into the fridge near the front and took out a small bottle. It looked expensive. The dark fluid sloshed around inside as he plopped it on the table.

"Now this is strong rum. We make it here at the resort and it can be a powerful drink."

Jessica and I smiled. "Alright sounds good. Pour me a cup!"

I took the still blunt of weed from the counter and inhaled. "Oh that stuff is strong!" I said, while taking another hit.

DeAndre chuckled while he dug out a cup from the kitchen area of the tower. "Careful, Mr. Johnson, that local weed can be a very potent aphrodisiac!"

"Hey DeAndre, you have any more of that weed?" Jessica asked.

DeAndre laughed. Wow you guys come into my tower and now you're drinking all my rum and using all my weed!" He joked. "Hold on let me see if I have any left."

DeAndre only poured half a drink before setting the glass down. He went near the counter to fetch another blunt of weed.

"Okay this is the only one I have left." DeAndre said as he

handed the blunt to Jessica. He lit it up and she smoked it in.
Her face sighed in relief as the affects of the plant took over.

"Alright, cheers to a great day!" I said while picking up
the glass. I downed it in one gulp.

"Wow he sure took that pretty fast didn't he."

"Yeah." Jessica said. I only took the shot a few moments
ago, but for some reason my hearing was a bit off. My head was
pounding. My muscles were getting tired and it was hard for me
to stand upright.

My vision deteriorated, but I could still hear the clutter
of voices in front of me.

"Hey is he going to be all right?"

"Yeah, he probably just drank the rum way too fast."

"Oh okay."

"Forget about your husband for now. I've been catching you
stare at me this entire trip..."

Before long, my eyes shut completely and I fell to the floor. Everything was black.

Chapter 3

I think I was on the couch or something. My eyes struggled to open all the way. My vision was still a little blurry. My hearing was fine though. I could make up the sound of moaning not too far away.

"You like my big black cock?"

"Oh yes! I love it!"

"How much do you love it?!"

"I've never had anything like it! I need to have more!"

"You like getting fucked in front of your husband, don't you my little slut?!"

"Yes!"

"Say it louder! I want to hear it!"

"I love it! I'm your white slut, DeAndre! I'll do anything! Please don't stop fucking my tight pussy!"

What was that I was hearing? My head was spinning. A strong
headache dulled my senses. My lips were dry and crackled as I
moved them. Strange, but familiar sounds filled my ears.

I heard the springs of a bed rocking back and forth.

"Mmmmmh!" Someone moaned very loudly.

"Oh you're a good little white whore for me!"

I heard flesh hitting flesh; the sound of passionate,
lustful lovemaking and moans.

I finally opened my eyes. A dark room greeted me. I stood
up and walked to the epicenter of that noise.

"Your white pussy is so fucking tight! I knew I had to have
your pussy when I first saw you."

"Oh!! Mmmmmh!" Someone moaned with deep pleasure.

"You like how I knocked out your husband don't you? You
like how I threw you on my bed don't you? You like my big black

cock!"

"Oh YES!!! I've never had anything like it!"

Now I remembered! DeAndre had just poured me a glass of rum and the next thing I knew I was out cold!

I moved up and around the corner to the other side of the room.

DeAndre was making love to my wife! He had just pulled out his cock and rammed it into her mouth.

"Oh yeah! Suck on my cock you white whore!"

My vision was coming into full focus. I saw Jessica on her knees on the bed with DeAndre standing at the edge.

He was thrusting his muscular body into her mouth in a rapid motion. I could hear Jessica gagging on his cock. She must have been practically choking.

I couldn't believe what I was seeing. DeAndre's cock was incredible. It was at least ten inches long. It put mine to shame for sure.

Jessica pulled his cock out of her mouth. An audible pop could be heard.

"Holy shit," I gasped, drawing their attention to me. DeAndre smiled at me. He wasn't surprised that I had walked into him fucking my wife like a little toy.

"Hello Jake, I'm just giving your wife some pleasure. She wanted my cock so bad, I couldn't deny her. I slipped a little medicine into your drink so I could make her dreams come true."

I felt sick in my stomach and nearly doubled over.

DeAndre stood up and placed his large hands on my shoulders, guiding me to a chair in front of the bed.

"Sit here and watch." He said in a soothing and calming voice.

I looked forward and saw his big cock dangling in front of me. He could have been mistaken for a horse. It looked so much bigger up close.

DeAndre took his position behind my beautiful wife. This was the moment it dawned on me that he wasn't wearing a condom! This hunky black guy was fucking my wife's unprotected pussy!

DeAndre inserted his large cock into my wife's sweet pussy. Her eyes rolled back as he slowly went in deeper and deeper.

I moved the chair forward so I was inches away from her face.

"His cock is so big! I've never felt anything like it!" She whispered to me as DeAndre fucked her hard.

"You're enjoying this?"

"I've always wanted black cock." She told me. "DeAndre is a god. His body is so hot; I just had to have him. Plus I think there was something in the weed."

I guess she was right. I wasn't actually pissed at them for this defilement of our marriage. I was more intrigued and turned on to be honest. Wow that must have been some really strong stuff DeAndre gave us.

"Uuuhhh! Mmmmmm!" Jessica moaned as DeAndre's cock ravaged her tight pussy.

"Is this what you want?"

"Yes!!"

"Tell your husband what you want!"

"I want DeAndre's big cock! I want his black cock so bad!"

I was on the edge of my seat now, my eyes glued to the action in front of me. I was frozen in place, unable to stop watching them perform magic.

DeAndre chuckled above.

"Hey Jessica, you want my big cock in your ass, don't you!"

"But it's too big!"

"I don't care! Beg me for it!"

"Please fuck my virgin ass DeAndre!"

Fuck her ass? He would destroy her tiny asshole!

"Tell your husband how much you want my cock in your ass!"

DeAndre grabbed the back of her neck forcibly and turned it towards me. It was the first time we made eye contact since I woke up.

"I want his cock in my ass." She said to me. Her eyes looked perplexed, like she was hypnotized or something. It must have been the weed.

"Jake...I need his cock."

I slid off the chair and dropped to my knees in front of her. Our faces only inches apart now. I leaned in to kiss her. I didn't care that DeAndre's big black horse cock was about to devour her ass.

I planted my lips firmly on hers. Our tongues danced with each other. She moaned into my mouth, biting on my lips. I tasted a bitter flavor. I realized that it was what black cock tasted like.

I held her head steady as DeAndre prepared his cock for her ass.

"Ready you little slut?"

Jessica nodded and DeAndre inserted the head into her ass. It barely fit in as Jessica moaned in pain or maybe it was pleasure. I couldn't tell.

"It's okay." I soothed her with my voice.

Eventually DeAndre fit his whole cock in her tiny ass. I couldn't believe it.

He began fucking her like a mad man. Jessica's head bobbled up and down.

"How is he?" I asked her.

"So GOOD!" She moaned. "It's so good! His cock is so uh so fucking big! I can't explain it babe. I just got so turned on. I need to taste his cock. I needed it in my pussy."

"Do you want his cum in you?" I blurted out. I couldn't believe I actually said that myself. For some reason the weed was making me really horny. DeAndre must have put some other extracts in there.

Jessica looked deeply into my eyes and we both knew what she wanted.

"I do. I want his cum so bad."

"You got one fucking tight hole white girl!" DeAndre remarked. "I've never fucked such a tight virgin ass before!"

"Uhhh!" Jessica responded as DeAndre picked up the speed. It must have been an indescribable feeling to have such a large cock penetrate her.

DeAndre slowed down for a moment and leaned forward. He grabbed my wife's hair and forced her head up to the ceiling.

"I'm going to cum in your ass, little whore!" DeAndre was breathing heavily from all that fucking.

Jessica licked her lips as she heard her lover's booming, dominant voice.

"Yes, please. That's what I want!"

"Louder! BEG!"

"YES! I want it! I want your load in me! Fill my ass!"

DeAndre chuckled at Jessica's response. He pulled his cock all the way back until only his large head remained in her ass.

Then in one fell motion, he jerked forward, pushing his entire ten inch cock into her ass once again.

Jessica screamed loudly as he came in her ass.

"OH GOD! I can feel it! I can feel every shot!" Jessica moaned in a delirious state of pleasure. If she wasn't so high right now, I would have thought she was possessed by some evil spirit.

DeAndre's large f dug into Jessica's arms, pinning her down completely as his orgasm reached its peak. He came deep inside her. Jessica had served his needs. She was just his little dirty cum dumpster.

DeAndre finally pulled out of her virgin ass. It was completely covered in his white cum. Cum gushed out of her ass, dribbling down to her pussy and legs. I was surprised she wasn't bleeding given how large his black cock was.

Jessica let out a big sigh of relief as his cock left her tight ass.

DeAndre walked around and pushed me to the side. He stood in front of my wife now, once again.

"Open your mouth, my whore!" He commanded her in a stern voice.

Jessica opened her mouth obediently without hesitation.

DeAndre slipped his prized cock into her mouth. "Suck my cum and your ass juices from my cock!"

My wife eagerly accepted DeAndre's gracious offering. She sucked on that black cock like it was the last thing she would ever do. She sucked every bit of cum off him.

Eventually DeAndre pulled out again. He chuckled to himself as he looked as us. He had turned my wife into his little ass fucking, cum sucking whore.

"Well, I hope you two had fun and enjoyed the rum and weed. Enjoy your stay at our resort."

DeAndre left us alone after that.

Jessica was completely drained of all her energy. The little fuck session had left her barely awake.

"Let's go back to our room," she said in a weak voice, while smiling at me.

I couldn't find her bikini anywhere, so I wrapped my wife in a towel and carried her out of the tower and back to our room.

As my feet hit the sand on the way down from the tower, I looked down at my new wife. Her body had just been fucked thoroughly by a big black cock and I knew this would not be the last time it would happen...

Taken By The Trainer

Jessie Sinclair

Copyright © 2017 Jessie Sinclair

All Rights Reserved

Chapter 1

I came home tired from today. A splitting headache followed me around. It had been a tough week. Our office manager, Tim, had turned into a real slave driver. He had set some impossible sales goals and we had fallen behind. There were only two months left in the year, so he had put the team into overdrive to achieve the goals. In essence, we've been working like slaves so he could collect a fat bonus from corporate.

It was a quarter past eight; I was already more than an hour late for dinner. I promised my wife, Holly, that I'd be home so we could spend some time together. Holly stopped in the office today to see if we could have a little impromptu lunch getaway. However, Tim vetoed the idea and I was stuck there

I felt bad, I wanted to spend some more time with Holly. I guess I had been neglecting her the past few weeks. It was my intent to make it up to her tonight. I showed up with her favorite flowers, pink roses.

Holly heated some leftovers for me. For some reason, she seemed oddly giddy tonight. I couldn't quite put my finger on it. After our late dinner, she dropped a bombshell on me.

"Someone asked me out today, George."

"Who?" Someone dared to ask out my wife?

"It was Russell."

"Who's that?"

"Russell? You know him. I've mentioned him a few times. He's my yoga instructor!"

It hit me like a bag of bricks. I remembered Holly said she signed up for a series of yoga classes a few weeks ago. But this guy actually had the audacity to ask her out? It pissed me off!

"I hope you told him to fuck off." I said crudely.

"Well...I told him I was married, but he just kept coming on."

"Do you want me to talk to this loser tomorrow?"

"Oh stop it. Don't be so jealous. We're just going to have

lunch tomorrow."

"What?! You actually said yes? What the hell were you thinking?" I gave my wife a death stare. Here I was working like a pig and she accepted some date with her yoga instructor?

"Relax babe! It's just lunch at a sandwich place; it's totally harmless."

"Well..."

"What? You don't trust me? I seem to remember letting you go to that strip club in Vegas for Dave's bachelor party. Besides you haven't exactly been romantic as of late..."

Dave was one of my good friends from college. About six months ago, we had a wild three-day weekend party in Vegas. It was an amazing time. I couldn't believe Holly brought that up. This was completely different! However, I decided to bite my tongue. I knew she already made up her mind.

"Fine just go, but he better not make any moves on you." I grumbled in defeat.

I went to bed slightly angry that night. Holly and I didn't even participate in our nightly cuddle ritual. I couldn't believe that my own wife had accepted a date with this mystery man. It just pissed me off. Who did that guy think he was?

The next morning, Holly and I didn't exactly speak. It was a little awkward to be honest.

I sat at my desk around noon for lunch. The guys and I ordered pizza from a local joint. However, all I thought about was Holly and her little rendezvous with Russell. I wondered what that little snot looked like. I bet I could pound his little head in. He was probably a little wuss.

I texted Holly to ask about the date. She responded to let me know she had just arrived at the restaurant. That was the last I heard from her.

Traffic was light on the way home. I hoped to see my wife when I got back. To my surprise, the driveway was empty. Hours passed and at around 9:00 P.M. I heard a car pull into our house. Holly walked in shortly after. My curiosity was killing me. However, I didn't want to give her the satisfaction of knowing I waited up for her.

My wife stumbled into our bed dead tired. Holly changed into a pair of shorts and a t-shirt and climbed into bed with me. I was absolutely livid, yet I didn't say anything. I felt her hands caress my bare chest. "Don't you want to know what I did today?"

"What? I thought you just went to a sandwich place." I shot back at her.

"Well we did...but it was so much fun we decided to go to happy hour down the street."

It was like being dropped out of a 10 story building. My heard nearly dropped out of my chest. She had drinks with this guy?

"What?"

"Yep, he bought me drinks...and he might have tried to make a move on me."

"What happened?"

"Well...we had a few shots and he was getting frisky. He pushed me up against the stall of the bathroom and we made out. It was so hot. He fingered me to two orgasms!"

I gasped in shock. Meanwhile, my wife's hands wandered down from my chest towards my waistline. She playfully pulled against the band of my boxers and let it snap back. For some reason, the thought of this guy making a move on my wife turned me on. The blood rushed to my lower body as I pictured his hands all over Holly.

Holly unbuttoned my boxers and slid her hand in. I felt the cool touch of her fingers against my warm cock. I was at full mast. She slowly jerked me underneath the blankets.

"I knew it! You love this!"

"No..." I tried to protest, but my cock betrayed me. I moaned softly as she continued to jerk me off.

"You love the thought of another man having me." She whispered seductively into my ear. Her lips caressed my outer lobe. I could feel her wet tongue sliding around in there. My body tingled with warmth and pleasure.

"Oh god!" I moaned.

Holly pulled the sheets to the side and straddled me. Her pink panties were wet to the touch. "Come fuck me, baby." She pulled her panties to the side, revealing her swollen pussy lips.

It was so weird, but I pushed my cock into her pussy. I had never seen Holly this wet before. She must have really had the hots for this guy.

"Oh yeah! That's it, baby!"

Holly bounced on my cock furiously. Our bodies slammed into each other at top speed as she rode my cock. I started to thrust upwards as well.

"There you go!!! Fuck me!"

"Mggh!" I grunted as my cock entered into her sweet pussy.

"That's it! Keep going!"

"You're such a fucking whore!" I grunted out at her. I don't know where that came from.

"Yeah! You know I am. I wanted his cock so bad there and then, but he had to run off."

"Oh yeah?"

Holly and I continued to fuck as she told me what really happened.

"Yeah, I could tell he had a fucking huge cock. It would have ripped my pussy apart!"

I felt her the walls of her tight cunt squeeze against me. It was such a hot situation. My dick strained inside her. I couldn't believe she wanted to fuck this guy!

"You did?!"

"Yeah! You know what? I'm going to call him tomorrow night! He's going to fuck my tight little pussy reaaaaal good! You'd like that wouldn't you, little cuck!"

There it was! She said it! Cuck...

Hearing Holly use that word pushed me over the edge. I grunted one last time as I passed the point of no return. I shot my seed deep into her pussy!

"Oh yeah! Cum in my pussy like Russell is going to do tomorrow!"

Holly reached her climax as I came in her. The walls of her pussy tried to push my cock out. It was the most powerful orgasm I had seen from her. Holly and I continued to rock against each other as our orgasms subsided.

We were both exhausted and panting from our oddly erotic love making session. Holly curled up against me and kissed me on the cheek. "That was amazing, baby."

"Yeah it was." I sighed.

"You know I love you, right?" She asked honestly.

"Yes, I know."

Soon after, we both passed out without another word being exchanged.

Chapter 2

The next morning, Holly had made waffles when I got into the kitchen for my daily coffee dose. She knew those were my favorite. My cock still throbbed from last night. It was the weirdest make-up sex I ever had.

"Hi babe! Did you sleep well?"

"It was good. Oh you made my favorite! Chocolate waffles."

"Anything for my hubby." She said with a smile.

"So...I called Russell this morning." My wife said.

"Oh really? W-what did you d-discuss?"

"Well, just wanted to see his schedule for the day. Was thinking about dropping in for a class. Plus...I wanted to see if he was open for dinner so we could continue from last night."

My cock nearly jumped after I heard that. The sex we had last night felt so right, yet so wrong. I couldn't quite place a finger on it.

"Oh...um okay." I said as I took a bite of the creamy
waffles.

My wife wrapped her hands around me as I continued to eat.
"Don't worry baby. I'll fuck him reeeeal good."

"You are?"

"Yeah...he's going to fuck me real good, cuck boy!" Holly
playfully jerked my cock off through my boxers and left to pack
my lunch.

It was hard to concentrate at work that day. The only thing
I imagined was Holly being bent at Russell's bachelor pad and
thoroughly fucked. I pretty much had a hardon all day at the
desk.

I managed to sneak out of work early. I promised Holly I
would check out her outfit before she went out on her hot date.

The door was unlocked when I got home. I walked upstairs to
the bathroom. Holly wore a strapless black cocktail dress and
some killer four inch matching heels. Her blonde hair had been

curled. It was a magnificent sight; like staring at an angel.

"How do I look, babe?"

Holly gave me a little twirl as her hair bounced around. I caught a whiff of her fragrant fruity shampoo that got the blood pumping downstairs.

"You look amazing babe!"

"Aww, you're so cute." Holly slapped me playfully on the cheek. "Now, you're going to be a good cuck and wait up for me tonight, aren't you!"

"Yes, I'll wait." I said with excitement. I couldn't believe this was happening. A few days ago I was livid at the thought of my wife going on a date with someone else. Now, I was looking forward to it!

"Okay, I'll be back before you know it. Try not to play with yourself too much." Holly tapped the bulge in my pants and walked out the door. I saw a red sports car pull up in the driveway. The windows were tinted so I couldn't see Russell's face. Holly smiled at the man and jumped in. The two sped off into the distance as I wondered how crazy things would get.

Almost as soon as they left, I texted Holly. I waited a few minutes for a response...nothing. I waited 10 minutes, then 30, then an hour. Still nothing. I became worried...what if this guy was a serial killer? Eventually it became too late and my eyes became heavy. I passed out after midnight.

At round 2:00 A.M. I heard the roar of a mighty engine down the street. It must have woken up the whole neighborhood! I jumped off the couch and looked out the window. It was the same sports car. My heart skipped a beat. I couldn't believe Holly was back.

The car just sat there in the driveway for a few moments. What in the world was going on? Then I noticed the car rocked back and forth. Oh god! Were they doing it in the car? After a few minutes, the passenger door opened and Holly emerged.

I couldn't get a good look at my wife because it was too dark out. The driver side door opened as well and a towering dark figure scooped up my wife in her hands as she screamed with glee. If the neighbors weren't up before, they would be now.

The two of them stumbled to the door. I could hear my wife giggle; she was obviously pretty tipsy. "Oh stop it, Russell! You're going to wake up the whole neighborhood!" My wife said, slurring her words.

"Let them watch then." He said in a cocky tone.

Holly's keys jingled as the door slammed open. She jumped out of his arms and walked towards me on the couch. "Well look who it is! He stayed up all night! I told you he would!"

My wife stroked my hair like she would a prized pup. "You must be George. I'm Russell." The giant black man said in a booming voice. He didn't even extend his hand out to shake.

I looked up at Russell and knew why my wife liked him immediately. He was 6'3" and built like a NBA player. He had broad shoulders and arms bigger than my legs. I couldn't even imagine how big his cock was. His jet black skin was darker than the night sky.

Holly stared at Russell for a moment. I knew exactly what she wanted. She looked back at me. "Baby, why don't you go pour us some wine."

"But..."

"No buts! Just do it." She commanded me in a stern voice.

I left for the kitchen. When I came back, Holly and Russell were making out passionately on the couch. They shed a few layers of clothes too. My wife's cocktail dress and Russell's shirt scattered on the floor.

"Um...here are your drinks." I must have looked like an idiot as this clearly superior man groped my wife.

The lovebirds only took a sip of wine before getting dirty again. My wife's hands moved all over his ripped body. Her dainty white hand contrasted against against his dark chest. I could see the outline of his hardon. Russell was a monster...

"Do you like it when Russell is kissing me?" Holly teased me.

"Yes." I nodded.

"Get on your knees and watch from below." She commanded me

with a giggle.

"What?" I hesitated for a moment until Russell barged into our conversation.

"You heard the lady! Drop to your knees, loser!" His voice echoed throughout our house.

He didn't have to tell me twice. I fell to my knees immediately.

"That's much better. Now I'm going to take his cock out for a spin and you're going to watch."

I nodded in response.

Holly unbuckled our black bull's pants and dropped his pants to the floor. All that remained between my wife and Russell was his briefs. I saw the fire in Holly's eyes. She desired nothing more than this big black man's cock. For some reason that's all I lusted for as well.

My wife slowly teased Russell by licking his cock through the briefs. She paid special attention to the head. He leaned back and moaned in pleasure.

"Yeahhhh! There you go, slut! I bet you've never had a cock as big as mine!"

Holly looked back at me and smiled. We both knew Russell was at least twice my size. "No, I haven't" She said with a big grin on her face.

"Take it out then. Suck on my cock."

My wife quickly pulled down Russell's briefs. His giant 12 inch cock sprung to action and almost hit her in the face. Holly was like a kid at the candy store. She couldn't believe the gift in front of her.

"Wow...it's so big." She slowly stroked his snake in amazement.

"Bitches all the same, never seen black cock." Russell said with a chuckle.

Holly planted her lips on Russell's bulbous head. She sucked down as Russell moaned. "Oh yeaaah! Your wife is a great cocksucker, George!" He slapped my wife on the ass as she grunted.

"Gag on it!" Russell grabbed the back of my wife's head and pounded her down. I was afraid he would her her, but I saw Holly rub her pussy below. I couldn't believe it! A big black man was using my wife like a sexy toy...like a common whore!

"Mmmmmm!" Holly groaned as she sucked on his cock. I never thought she could take something as big as that!

"That's a good whore! Show your loser husband what a cunt you are!"

Holly tried to escape his cock to catch a breath, but Russell wouldn't let her. I saw my wife's face turn blue as she chocked on his member. After a few more thrusts, Russell pushed her head off his cock.

My wife gasped for air as Russell chuckled like a king on his throne. "How did my cock taste." He laughed.

"Amazing!" Holly replied.

"Sit on my lap. I want to fuck your tight cunt."

Holly sat on his lap as instructed. My wife was naked except her bra and panties. It was a sight to see. Russell gripped my wife's breasts in his and squeezed. "Yeah, these are nice tits."

He ripped off the bra and revealed Holly's diamond hard nipples. Russell sucked on them like a baby. My wife moaned in response.

"Oh god! Fffffuck me Russell!"

"You hear that, loser? Your wife wants me to fuck her."

"Yes, I heard it." I said calmly. My cock was rock hard in my pants. Everything about this night was so wrong, but I had never been more turned on in my life.

"I think you should beg me to tear your wife's pussy! Come on, wimp! Let me hear it!"

"Please fuck my wife, sir." I said with a shaky voice.

"I'm not convinced. Beg me harder!"

"Please fuck her Russell! Your cock can please her in ways I can't!"

Russell laughed at my desperation. It must have looked pretty pathetic.

"Very well. I'm going to fuck your wife, loser!"

Russell guided his cock into my wife's holy temple. Holly gasped as his head rubbed against her clit. "Oh!" She moaned softly. I couldn't believe he was going to put that monster in my wife.

Holly's lips trembled as Russell's cock went deeper and deeper. She screamed in a mix of pleasure and pain. Her pussy clung to his cock in a tight wrap.

"Oh yeah you're fucking tight slut! Bet you've never had black cock before!"

"Never!"

"Good! I like taking your black cock virginity!"

Russell looked at me with a cocky smile. "By the time I'm done with your wife, she won't be the same again. You'll never enjoy her stretched pussy. The only cock she'll crave will be black cock!"

His words burned into my head. I couldn't believe what was about to happen to my wife!

Russell grabbed my wife's hips and rocked back and forth. Every thrust pushed my wife into a state of pure pleasure. Holly groaned in like an animal. I've never seen her like that before.

"It's so big! Oh my god! My husband is not like this!"

"You like that?!"

"Yes, Russell! I've never been so satisfied like this before!" My wife screamed deliriously like a mad woman as Russell pounded her tight pussy. I was afraid his cock would split Holly in two.

"That's right bitch! I'm going to fill up your pussy with

my cum!"

"Oh god yes! Please! Yes! Do it!!"

My cock throbbed as I watched my wife beg Russell for his cum.

Russell slammed his cock into her over and over and over. Her boobs jiggled with each thrust. His cock ravaged her pussy. I knew she would never be the same again.

"Here it comes you whore!"

Russell took a deep breath before he completely exploded in my wife. I could literally see his cock throb with pleasure as his seed filled my wife.

"God! Fill me up!" My wife screamed at the top of her lungs and succumbed to her own intense orgasm.

Russell pushed my wife to the couch next to her after he was done. They both panted in exhaustion. I saw Russell's black seed run out of my wife's pussy and drip to the floor.

"What are you waiting for, cuck? Clean my TOY for me!" Russell gave me a death stare to show he meant business.

I didn't dare disobey him. I crawled between my wife's legs. Her pussy lips were swollen and probably sore. I suck on her folds, savoring a mixture of her sweet pussy and the bitter taste of black cum.

Holly moaned ans held the back of my head firmly. "Oh yeah! Clean his mess up, baby!"

Meanwhile, Russell stood up and put his pants on. As he buckled his belt, he looked down at me. "You better clean that pussy real good cause I'm not having any kids, understand me?"

"Yes sir." I said in a meek voice.

"Good cuck." Russell then looked at my wife and smiled. "I'll pick you up tomorrow night. We're going to have more fun." He said matter-of-factly."

Holly and I fucked again that night. Her pussy was different...it was too big now. Russell's words about ruining her burned into the back of my mind. Holly cupped my face. "Did you have fun, baby?"

"Yes, it was amazing."

"Great, because I can't wait to fuck him again tomorrow."

Holly and I fell asleep together on the couch. As I passed out, there was only one thing on my mind: I knew our marriage and sex life would never be the same again.

Taken On The Cruise

Jessie Sinclair

Copyright © 2017 Jessie Sinclair

All Rights Reserved

Chapter 1

It was a beautiful afternoon aboard the Disney Dream cruise ship. Not a single cloud formed across the vast skyline. The blue ocean waves lightly pushed against the hull of the ship. A slight sway could be felt. The hot Florida sun blazed down on all the passengers.

Tom and Jennifer just walked up to their expensive first class suite. The two of them secured a room near the top of the ship. The view couldn't be any better. It was nearly sunset. The sun had begun to turn orange as it prepared to sleep for the night.

Tom hoped tonight would be a night of romance...a night to remember...a night to look forward to.

The two late twenty-year olds have been married for only a short year. Things had been a bit rocky for their marriage so far, unfortunately.

You see...Tom just couldn't please his wife. Jennifer needed a big cock to get her to orgasm. Her husband's little three inch dick just would not get the job done.

They tried everything. Jennifer got him to try a penis pump, but it only enlarged Tom's little pecker by a few inches.

They tried using a strapon, but it didn't make her wet. Jennifer needed the real thing; she needed flesh. She needed to feel the hard skin of a large cock ram into her tight little pussy to get off.

For the better half of the past year, Jennifer had been totally unsatisfied by her husband. She loved him very much and they were great friends. They cared for each other deeply.

However, a woman just needs to be pleased in the bed sooner or later. The two went to couples counseling and sex classes to help train Tom to be a better lover in the bedroom.

It worked to a certain extent. He learned to be quite proficient with his mouth. However, it was hard work for Tom to get her off.

He would often in excess of half an hour with his tongue just to get her off. He had hoped that this romantic cruise would spark something between them.

The two lovebirds had just entered into the room. Tom had made sure the staff lit candles and sprinkled rose petals on the floor.

"Oh wow! This room is so nice; it's so romantic!" Jennifer exclaimed and sighed as she took in the beautiful view of the ocean.

Tom dropped their bags next to the bed and walked over to the side window. He wrapped his arms over his wife and pushed aside her shoulder-length blonde hair. He slowly brought his lips to the back of her neck and kissed softly.

"You like the view?"

Jennifer brought her hands to Tom's and they embraced.

"It's lovely," she whispered back.

Tom lowered his mouth toward her left hear. "Hey, what do you say we make love while the sun sets?"

To be honest, Jennifer knew what Tom was trying to do with

this whole vacation. She knew he was trying to sweep her off her feet.

She appreciated the effort, but there was only one thing that would satisfy her: a big cock. Jennifer played along though; she didn't want to hurt Tom's feeling too bad.

"Yeah sure, let's give it a try."

Jennifer turned around and the two locked lips. Tom could taste the smeared texture from her fruity lip gloss. He just had to have more.

Tom guided his wife towards the bed and lightly pushed her backwards. Jennifer smiled as Tom removed his belt. Meanwhile, she began stripping as well.

Soon enough both husband and wife were naked in bed with the sun as the only witness of their love. Tom was fully erect at this point.

He planted a few kisses on Jennifer's knee. He moved up slowly towards her pussy. She had just shaved it the other day, so not a single strand of hair lived.

Tom placed his lips on her pussy and sucked softly.
Jennifer began to moan in pleasure. It was of course a facade.
There wasn't enough foreplay to get her really wet.

She just went along not to hurt his feelings. Tom went down
on her for a few minutes while Jennifer's mind wandered.

Before long it was the moment she dreaded. Tom sat up on
his knees between her legs. He moved to lie on top of his wife.

Jennifer felt her breasts compress against his chest. Her
nipples, unlike her husband's cock, were totally soft.

She felt his little three inch cock circle around her pussy
lips. Tom tried his best to tease Jennifer. He rubbed his cock
all around her pussy. His precum smeared around, allowing it to
move more freely.

Little did he know his cock was one of the last things his
wife wanted right now. In her head Jennifer was thinking about
what they would be doing later.

Jennifer moaned and panted as Tom tried to work his magic.

He inserted his pin dick into her pussy. To be frank, she didn't even feel it go in.

Tom began thrusting. Their hips connected as he fucked her as hard as he could. Tom moaned in pleasure, while Jennifer had to pretend.

After a few more minutes Jennifer had enough. She couldn't keep going anymore. Her husband just wasn't getting the job done.

She held the back of Tom's head. "Hey, um...let's continue this later. It was great foreplay, but I'm kind of hungry. Let's go down to the restaurant and eat...maybe dance a little after that and then continue this."

A shade of disappointment appeared on Tom's face, but it faded after a few moments. He had the entire three-day weekend to please his wife, so a little delayed gratification wouldn't hurt too much.

"U-um, yeah sure. Let's go."

The two got dressed and headed down to the elevator.

Chapter 2

Tom and Jennifer headed out of the elevator into the restaurant on the fourth floor. It was an upscale place. While eating, Jennifer thumbed through her phone looking for fun activities.

She really wanted to dance. Luckily the cruise had a nightclub/lounge on the fifth floor. It would be perfect.

"Hey, what do you say we go dancing after we eat?"

Dancing? Tom thought about it for a second. Well, if it would get Jennifer more aroused then he would totally be up for it.

"Yeah let's do it. Sounds like fun."

Tom and Jennifer quickly ordered at the restaurant. As dinner came to a close, Tom grabbed his wife's purse as they left.

The sky had darkened and the cool ocean breeze brushed against their skin. It was a beautiful night. A few clouds scattered across the horizon.

The two of them ascended through the elevator for the nightclub. As soon was the doors opened, both of them could hear the music blaring.

They walked up the stairs and were greeted by a large bouncer.

"May I see your I.D please," he said with a deep voice. Tom and Jennifer pulled out their licenses and he stamped their wrists.

"Enjoy, have a good night."

The bars of the club were lit with colorful neon lights. Hundreds of other fellow passengers were getting drunk and having the time of their lives.

To the right of the club stood the executive lounge. It was lined with a dozen or so black leather couches and tables. The bar stood across the entire back side of the room.

"Hey, do you want to grab a drink?" Tom said. He had hoped

a little liquid courage would help arouse Jennifer for their later bedroom activities.

"Yeah sure. Let's go."

Tom and Jennifer joined hands and headed for the bar.

They quickly ordered a round of drinks; a vodka soda for Jennifer and a beer for Tom. The two quickly walked around the room.

"Do you want to dance?" Tom said, trying to be as romantic as he could.

Jennifer agreed and they headed down to the dance floor.

Tom held Jennifer from the back as she grinded against him. It didn't take long for him to get hard. She could feel his three inch dick pushing back against her ass.

"Oh god," thought Jennifer. She couldn't do another round of sex later this evening--if what they experienced was even sex for that matter.

After a few minutes Tom needed to use the bathroom. "Hey babe, I've got to hit the head. I'll be right back."

"Okay. I'll wait for you in the lounge. I need to rest for a bit anyways; my legs are a bit tired."

"Okay. I'll be right out and then we can continue this." He leaned forward and kissed her on the lips.

Jennifer headed to the lounge and plopped down on one of the comfortable couches.

"Tired from dancing too much?" A deep and sexy voice penetrated Jennifer's ears.

She turned around and saw the most handsome man she had ever seen sit down next to her. This man was built like a Greek god. His muscles popped out of his tight t-shirt. She could see every curve on his biceps.

His black skin glistened under the dimmed lights of the room. His chiseled jaw smiled at Jennifer. Her heart melted when she saw that he made eye contact.

Jennifer felt butterflies in her stomach. Her face must have turned red that this god was even paying attention to her.

"O-oh...u-um yeah. I was a bit tired from dancing."

"Too tired? That's no fun. A beautiful angel like you would be the belle of the ball on the dance floor."

"Oh stop it, now you're just trying to embarrass me."

"No I'm not." This man said. His deep, commanding voice somehow hypnotized her.

"Come on get up, I'm going take you back to dance."

The man stood up and towered over Jennifer. He must have been at least 6'4". He extended his hand out.

Jennifer hesitated for a second. "I uh probably shouldn't. My husband just in the bathroom."

"Your husband?"

"Yes," she replied, "plus I don't even know you.

The man took a look at Jennifer before he responded. "I'm Marshawn. What's your name?"

"It's Jennifer." She wasn't sure where he was going with this.

"Well Jennifer, I'm going to ask you something...does your man satisfy you?"

"What? Of course he does! He takes good care of me. I have a great roof over my head, expensive clothes on my back, and this great vacation."

"Oh I wasn't talking about that." He said with a seductive voice. Jennifer felt weak to her knees already. This man had some kind of unexplainable pull on her emotions.

"What do you mean?"

"I mean does he satisfy you in the bedroom?"

"What? Why in the world would you ask that?"

"Well I saw you dance with your husband. Your mind seemed to be somewhere else. You were barely touching him. And right now, I can tell how horny you are. I can basically smell it off you. You haven't been satisfied in a while."

Jennifer sat there in a little bit of shock. She couldn't believe Marshawn had figured her out like that.

"I u-um..."

"Don't say anything at all. Come with me and I'll show you how a real man dances with a woman like you."

There was just something about Marshawn that compelled Jennifer to go with him. She took his hand and he lifted her effortlessly.

His large, manly hands wrapped around hers easily. Before she knew it Jennifer was on the dance floor with Marshawn.

He grabbed her waist from behind and grinded up against her ass. Jennifer's nipples became hard for the first time in years. She felt Marshawn's fingers caress her skin. She felt his lips pressed against the back of her neck.

His lips whispered into her ear. "I bet you've never experienced anything like this before in your life."

Jennifer could smell the manly scent of his cologne. It filled her nose and she became even more infatuated with this mysterious man.

"Oh!" Jennifer moaned softly. "I've never felt like this before."

Her pussy was tingling. It was almost a foreign sensation. Tom never made her feel anything like his before. She shook her ass harder and faster.

Eventually, she could feel Marshawn's cock begin to harden. It felt so big...like he literally had a snake in his pants. She couldn't believe what she was rubbing up against.

"Oh my god, how big is your cock?"

"Don't worry you'll find out soon enough."

"Wait? What about Tom?" Jennifer thought. She had never

felt this way and wanted more. She had to have more. She had to have her orgasm...

Chapter 3

Tom exited the bathroom. It had taken him way too long. Apparently someone had thrown up all over the urinals. The staff had to close part of it down to clean up.

He wasn't too happy about that. All Tom wanted to do again was get back to the lounge and dance with Jennifer. He left the bathroom after almost peeing in his pants from waiting so long.

Back at the lounge Tom couldn't spot his sexy wife anywhere. He looked around at the bar, but still nothing. He was getting a bit worried. Maybe she went back up to their room?

He took out his phone and texted her.

-Where are you?-

He waited a few minutes, but nothing. Tom decided to go check out the club and see if she had somehow stumbled there.

He surveyed the entire club and finally honed in on is wife. What Tom saw terrified him. Jennifer was dancing with some large black guy!

What in the world was she doing? He walked up to them and pulled them apart.

"Jennifer, who is this guy? Why were you dancing with him?"

Marshawn stood there in front of Tom and Jennifer with a calm demeanor to his face. He was clearly the superior alpha man in every single aspect.

Tom was about four inches shorter and lacked the same muscle Marshawn boasted. He would be no match in the animal kingdom.

Jennifer was put in an awkward situation. "Oh um Tom...this is Marshawn. We just met while you were in the bathroom."

"What?"

"He's going to take me up to our room. I want to fuck him. He's got a big dick. I need to fuck him. I haven't cum since I've met you."

Tom couldn't believe what he was hearing.

"I...I...I'm not sure..."

"Don't worry, I still love you. I just need his cock. Yours will never get the job done." Suddenly Jennifer's tone of voice became more dominant. Marshawn's attitude must have rubbed off on her.

"I um...b-but..." Tom knew the truth. He had been trying to use his cock to satisfy his wife for a long time and nothing worked.

Maybe it would be better to let Marshawn do it. Wait a minute! This all sounded so crazy! Let another man fuck his wife--especially one as handsome and built as Marshawn?

"Yes, you're going let him fuck me. In fact, you're going to watch it and like it. I might let you in me after I cum on his cock."

Jennifer smiled at her husband and walked past to Marshawn who had been eavesdropping on the entire private conversation.

"Come on babe, I want your hard cock in me."

Marshawn smiled and pulled Jennifer in and kissed her on the lips. Tom could barely stomach himself as he watched another man make out with his wife. He almost threw himself in the middle as he saw Marshawn rub his enormous hands all over her shoulders.

After the brief kiss, the two new lovebirds held hands and headed upstairs.

In the elevator Marshawn pinned Jennifer against the wall and forced his lips on hers. Tom couldn't do anything, but watch their chemistry unfold.

Jennifer's breathing became more and more labored. Marshawn bit down on her lip and she nearly lost it. Tom could never please her like that.

Soon enough the trio were near their room. All of a sudden Marshawn picked up Jennifer like they were newlyweds crossing the threshold.

"Hey tell your little cuck boy to open the door for us." His voice boomed across the hall. If anyone was around they would have surely heard that remark.

"You heard him babe. Open the door."

Tom just accepted his fate. He hated the situation; it was
so humiliating. However, he also wanted Jennifer to get off.

He pulled out the room key from his back pocket and scanned
it. Marshawn forcibly kicked open the door with his right foot
and carried her through.

As he entered, Marshawn threw Jennifer on the bed as she
screamed in delight. He jumped up as well, landing above her.

"You want my big cock don't you? Your husband's little
white boy cock will never satisfy you."

Wow, Tom couldn't believe Marshawn was humiliating him like
that with such bravado.

"Yeah, his little pindick is so tiny."

"Oh yeah? Tell him to show us."

"Hey Tom! Pull down your pants. We want to see your tiny dick."

Tom knew he was going to regret it, but he did it anyways. He dropped his pants and his little dick hung in the air.

Marshawn burst out laughing. "Wow! I guess it's true what they say about white boys. No wonder you haven't cum in ages."

Jennifer nodded her head. "You have no idea. I need your cock so bad."

Marshawn knew exactly what Jennifer wanted. He grabbed at her shirt and tore it apart. She was surprised at how strong he was.

Next, Marshawn slipped off her bra and revealed her hard nipples. He leaned in and gave her a kiss on the lips. His teeth grazed her full red lips as Jennifer shuddered in pleasure she'd never felt before.

"Oh god!" She moaned.

Marshawn moved his lips down her neck until they were

between her breasts. He grabbed onto them both and squeezed, forcing her nipples to become even harder.

Jennifer pulled her head back against the pillows. Marshawn plowed his lips down and sucked on her nipples, nibbling here and there.

Her legs spasmed with pleasure. Her pussy was wet.

Meanwhile, Tom could only watch as his wife was being pleasured. He couldn't do anything about it.

Tom saw his wife's big bull lift her by the waist. Marshawn pulled down the zipper on her pants and slipped them off. He threw them over his shoulder, nearly hitting Tom in the face.

"How wet is your pussy you little slut."

"Oh god so wet! So wet Marshawn. I've never felt a man like you!"

"Oh you'll feel me soon enough." He pressed his fingers against her pussy. Jennifer was wet for sure.

He held his finger out for Tom to see. "You see this, little dick boy? You would never be able to make your wife feel like that. Come kneel down here and watch me fuck her the right way."

Tom hesitated. He couldn't do that! He had to hold everything in not to go and try to tackle Marshawn. Wait...who was he trying to kid? Marshawn would be able to throw him across the room with ease. He was superior in every single way.

"You heard him babe. Kneel down and watch us fuck!"

Tom obeyed. He didn't know what was right and what was wrong anymore. He just knew he had to listen to his wife and let this play out.

As soon as Tom knelt down Marshawn pulled off her panties. Her pussy was so wet. It was like she had just showered.

Tom couldn't even believe what he saw. He never made Jennifer feel like that. Maybe it was best to let this superior black man defile his wife.

"How much do you want my cock!"

"More than anything!" She bellowed.

"Beg!"

"Please fuck me Marshawn!"

"Beg harder. I'm not convinced." He said in his deep commanding voice.

"Please fuck me with your cock! I need it so bad! I haven't cum in ages!"

"What do you think little cuck boy? Should I fuck your wife?"

"Yes, please pleasure her." Tom couldn't believe the words that just escaped his mouth. He saw how turned on Jennifer was and just couldn't say no.

"Alright then, let's go."

Marshawn pulled off his shirt and began to unbutton his pants. He pulled off his jeans and threw them at the floor next to Tom.

He pulled out his large cock. It must have been at least ten inches long.

Tom and Jennifer had never seen a cock so magnificent. His cock put porn stars to shame. It was truly a sight to behold.

"Oh my god. You're so big."

"Yeah. This big black cock is going to pound your tight little pussy."

Marshawn pushed his head against Jennifer's pussy lips.

"Oh!" She moaned with pleasure.

Marshawn rubbed his head against her clit in circles, teasing her. Her pussy juices lubed up is hard cock. He was ready to go.

He went in slowly. The first two inches were the hardest for Jennifer. Her pussy had never felt a cock so large. Tom could only watch in devastation and nervousness as her lover's horse-sized cock penetrated deeper and deeper.

Eventually Marshawn fully inserted his large black cock.

Jennifer moaned out in a mix of pleasure and pain. "God! Fuck me! Fuck me Marshawn! Fuck me like my husband never could!"

"That's right you little slut! You're going to love my dick!"

Marshawn moved forward, going into full missionary. His teeth bit down on her neck as he rammed his cock in and out.

"Oh god!"

Tom wished he could cover his ears. He only wished he could pleasure Jennifer like this, but he knew his tiny dick would never get the job done.

Marshawn and Jennifer locked lips as he fucked her. Every single movement of his cock sent shivers down to her clit. His cock was so big it hit her g-spot every single time.

With his lips pressed against hers, Jennifer's moans were

muffled. Her orgasm was coming near.

She pulled back to let them know. "I'm going to cum! Oh god! Keep going! Please!"

Marshawn picked up the speed. He could feel her pussy tighten.

"Oh! I'm cumming!" Her voice turned higher and higher until she shrieked like a banshee.

Jennifer convulsed for the first time in years. Her pussy wrapped harder around Marshawn's hard cock.

She began panting like an exhausted dog. Her chest lifted up with every breath.

"Please I need more. Please don't stop!"

"Oh I'm not stopping until I get off. Get on your knees."

Marshawn forced Jennifer to her knees on the bed with her ass in the air. He fingered her ass while he re-inserted his dick.

This time he wasn't so nice. He just rammed it in fast. He knew she could take it.

Doggy was one of Tom's favorite positions, so this was especially hard for him to watch.

Marshawn fucked her from behind. His large balls slapped against Jennifer's ass with every thrust. The sound was so loud Tom was afraid their neighbors across the hall would be able to hear.

That paled in comparison to Jennifer's screams though. She had never experienced ecstasy like this before.

Marshawn's cock felt every crevice of her pussy. Jennifer was near her second orgasm. "Agh! Keep going! You are a god!" She bellowed.

Marshawn picked up the pace again. His balls slammed against her ass rhythmically. Jennifer shuddered again as her second orgasm came.

She felt her entire body tingle in pleasure. "Oh!!!" She

screamed. Her pussy convulsed again as her head arched back towards the ceiling.

"I need your cum in me! Cum in my pussy!"

"I will, but only on one condition!"

"Name it!"

"Your little cuck boy has to lick it up!"

"Wait what?" Tom knew this had gone too far at this point.

"He'll do it!" Jennifer blurted out.

"What?"

"You'll do it because I said so!"

Tom was like a dog with his tail between his legs. He was utterly reduced to a little cuckold bitch slave.

"Alright, get on your back, slut!"

Marshawn waited until she was on her back again before jamming his cock in again. He was on top of her and trusted his large black cock in.

"Oh god! Oh god! Oh god!" It was the only thing Jennifer could comprehend at this point.

"You want my cum?"

"Yes! Please!"

"Here it comes!"

Marshawn trust a few more times. The cum was building up in his large balls.

"I'm going to cum in your pussy!"

His large cock spurt cum out like a super volcano. Jennifer spasmed. Marshawn's lava warm cum had caused her to orgasm for a third time!

Marshawn's cock spurt cum over and over again into her pussy. Eventually he pulled it out and it drizzled down.

"Oh god! Thank you!" She said between her panting.

Marshawn began getting dressed while Tom was shocked beyond belief. Marshawn reached into his pocket and pulled out a card.

"Here's my number. Call me again if you want to experience pleasure again." He left it on the nightstand before leaving.

"Are you okay babe?"

Jennifer could barely speak at this point. "Oh god that was so incredible!"

"I can't believe you did that."

"Don't worry babe. It was just a onetime thing. I want you to clean my pussy now. Clean his cum."

"Okay if it makes you happy." Tom said in a defeated voice.

He lowered his head and commenced the humiliating task. Meanwhile Jennifer pulled the card from the stand and sniffed it.

She could still smell Marshawn's cologne on the card. She thought about when she would see him next...

Nicole's Bitch Slave

Jessie Sinclair

Copyright © 2017 Jessie Sinclair

All Rights Reserved

Chapter 1

When I first met Nicole six months ago everything was great. I met her at a local cocktail party. When I first laid eyes on her I thought I saw an angel. She wore a fancy black cocktail dress. Her hair rolled straight down to her shoulders.

She wore a beautiful shade of velvet red lipstick. I was pretty nervous, but decided to approach her that night. We really hit things off from the beginning and I got her number at the end of the night. Not long after that we had our first date, which would turn into numerous other dates.

Life seemed great or so I thought. Three months in, Nicole still hadn't let me have sex with her. I know...crazy right? I tried to respect her privacy, but a guy's got to get some at some point! I waited another month and still nothing.

The craziest thing we did was make out...fully clothed. I know...so stupid. I wondered why she didn't want to have sex with me, but didn't have the courage to approach her on the subject. I thought that with extra time she would loosen up again and I'd finally get in her pants.

Well, another month passed and still nothing. I was beginning to get desperate at that point. Anyways, that was around the time Nicole started taking over our relationship.

She started ordering me around more. I did all the chores in our condo...that I paid for. She didn't even chip in one cent! She totally used my lust for her pussy against me. I didn't like how she used me like that, but I really wanted to get in her pants so I played ball.

Well that's when things got so much worse. Nicole began controlling every part of my life. She took over my bank accounts and my credit cards. I even have to ask her to use my own credit card whenever I have to buy something! It was absolutely ludicrous!

Anyways, I confronted her about this a month ago and she totally destroyed me...it was THAT bad. Nicole told me she bad collected blackmail evidence on me.

She had pictures of me naked that I sent her when we first started going out. She threatened to send them to everyone at my work if I didn't do what she said.

She completely took over my bank accounts and changed all the passwords. I couldn't even access my financials anymore. Nicole told me that if I didn't serve as her bitch slave she would totally ruin me.

I believe her. She seemed pretty crazy. She even sent a naked picture of me to my best friend, Ricky as proof that she wasn't kidding around. I was able to rationalize that text with him, but that wouldn't work at work. I'd probably get fired.

Nicole told me that from here on out, I was to serve her every single need...and that's what I did. For the last month I've been slaving for her hardcore. I've been working my ass off to make her monthly earnings quota. Meanwhile, she didn't even contribute to our condo payments!

Instead, she just lounged around all day and partied with her friends at night. I'd serve as her foot slave as well. That meant I would attend to her feet every single night. I would massage them, lick them clean with my tongue, and rub lotion on them.

She also locked me in a steel chastity cage. It has been so humiliating. Nicole totally has control of my dick. She hasn't let me cum since she locked me in that horrible cage...and that was a month ago! She's been using my horny libido against me.

I've been her stupid slave since then. It's like she has some kind of weird unexplainable control over me. I can't break out of it. I'm in WAY too deep. And that brings me to where I am right now...

I'm kneeling naked on the floor in front of the sofa in our living room (well I guess it's her living room now even though I pay for everything). Nicole had just walked in after going to lunch with her girlfriends.

"Hey slave looks like you're just where I left you."

"Yes, Princess Nicole." Oh yeah...I forgot to tell you, she ordered me to call her "Princess" from now on. Go figure, right?

She finished taking off her shoes while I wondered how she was going to abuse me now.

"So listen, slave. I have a hot date with my new boyfriend tonight. I'm going to do some shopping online at Victoria's Secret to make sure my wardrobe is full of sexy lingerie for him."

"What? New boyfriend?"

I didn't know she was even seeing anyone else. I felt so
betrayed by her.

Nicole seemed annoyed at my comment. She walked up to me
and slapped me hard in the face. I'm sure my cheek turned bright
red the moment her hand made contact.

"Yeah, I've been seeing someone else and he's much more of
a man than you are."

She really emphasized what a feeble man I was by rubbing my
locked up chastity dick with her barefoot.

"Yes, Princess! I am sure he is!"

"Now, that's a much better attitude, slave. Get on all
fours I need to use you as a footrest."

"Yes, Princess. As you wish."

I fell to my hands and knees as Nicole sat on the couch. She put her feet on my back as she reached over to open her laptop.

"So...what do you think Dan will like?" She said while laughing at me.

"I'm sure you look hot in anything, Princess."

"Yeah, at least you got that right, bitch."

"Okay, let's see what's new here. You did earn a decent wage this month, so I'll be spending extra on my new lingerie!"

"Yes, Princess. Thank you Princess. I worked so hard for you."

"As you should be. You're a fucking slave after all."

After about ten minutes, Nicole had surprisingly compiled a large list of items she wanted. She was really good at spending my money.

"Alright, slave. I'm ordering now. It'll be $536.46 Ha Ha!

God I love fucking using you as a pay piggy! You and your locked up dick are so fucking pathetic."

"Yes, Princess. Thank you for using me."

"And guess what slave? You're never going to have the satisfaction of fucking me in all this hot new lingerie I just bought! No...You're just going to be teased when I wear them."

Nicole stood back up after she had bought what she wanted. "Follow me to the bathroom, slave. You're going to help me get ready for my hot and sexy date..."

Chapter 2

"Kneel here on the floor." Nicole pointed her index finger at the floor in front of the shower.

I obeyed and saw her tower over me. She began taking off her clothes in front of me. She started off her pink top. She wore a sexy black bra underneath. My dick was already straining in its cage at this point. I felt as if it would burst out at any moment.

Next, Nicole removed her jeans and revealed a pair of purple panties. They wrapped around her ass perfectly. I wanted to taste so bad. She moved up to me and put her hands on my shoulders as she looked down and smiled.

"You like what you see, slave?" She emphasized "slave" by bringing her foot up and teasing my locked up dick.

"Yes, Princess. You are so beautiful."

"Well, it's too bad you won't be enjoying this sexy body tonight."

Nicole slapped me lightly on the cheek and laughed. She slowly removed her bra and her natural 34DD breasts fell out and bounced in the air. She never let me play with them even when I wasn't her slave. I wanted to touch them so bad and suck on her nipples.

Her sexy bra dropped to the floor as she put her hands on the panties that wrapped around her waist.

She brought them down slowly showing her perfectly shaved pussy. Her lips looked so smooth and soft. I really wanted to fuck her, but she never gave me that chance.

"Here, smell what you're going to be missing tonight."

Nicole put her panties over my face. She was cruel and put the still wet crotch portion directly over my nose. I inhaled the smell of her sweet pussy. It was still so moist and warm. My dick strained against the cage. The teasing was borderline unbearable.

"Oh, look! Someone's trying to get hard!"

Nicole kicked my balls again lightly. I closed my eyes and

groaned in pleasure from her teasing.

"Hold out your hands slave."

I held out both of my hands and Nicole dropped her towel into them.

"Keep your hands out like that while I'm showering. And don't think about even dropping those panties from your ugly face. If you're not in this position when I get out, there will be hell to pay."

"Yes, Princess. I understand."

"Good."

Nicole slid open sliding door and entered the tub. I heard the water turn on. I couldn't see through the class very well. Her panties had blocked part of my sight, plus the glass wasn't really that transparent anyways.

I continued to kneel there. I smelled her panties a few times while she cleaned herself. It seemed like she was taking forever to take her shower.

After what seemed like twenty minutes Nicole finally emerged from the shower. Water dripped from her amazing body as she took her towel from my outstretched hands.

"Okay, you're getting a treat today, slave! You get to dry me off, but no touching me with your disgusting bare hands. Got it?"

"Yes Princess. Thank you, Princess."

"You better do a good job." Nicole took her panties off my face and threw her towel back at me.

I started with her feet first. She had perfectly pedicured purple toes. I dried them off and moved up to her legs. I couldn't really feel her skin because of the towel. I guess that's what she wanted. I moved up to her pussy and ass and dried both.

My dick tugged against the cage. I was trying to get so hard, but it was utterly futile. Nicole just continued to laugh at me.

"Okay, you're so fucking pathetic slave! That's enough. I'm afraid you'll burst out of your birdie cage."

I was disappointed, but she called the strings so I stopped. "Yes, Princess. Thank you."

"Kneel down again."

Nicole finished drying herself up.

"Here, lie down on the floor in front of the sink."

I put my back against the cold marble floor. The next thing I knew, Nicole stepped on my chest and stomach. Her soft and silky feet pressed against my body. My dick went into overdrive. It tried so hard to get out of the cage, but nothing would work.

Even the touch of her feet drove me insane. That's how long I've been locked up.

"Stay still. I need to dry my hair."

"Yes, Princess."

Nicole took about ten minutes to dry her hair completely. I looked up and I saw her pussy. It was so beautiful. It glistened against the light from the ceiling. Nicole saw me checking her out and just chuckled.

She brought out her curling iron. Her hair looked fantastic after she finished it. Her curls bounced around at her every move. Nicole really did look like an angel. It's too bad she would never let me fuck her.

"Okay, slave...ready to help me put on my dress?"

"Yes Princess. Thank you for allowing me such an honor."

Nicole pulled out a sexy red cocktail dress from the counter. "Put it on and try not to screw anything up."

I took the dress from her. The material felt so soft. I unzipped the back and helped Nicole put it on. I rezipped the back and she twirled around in the mirror.

"How do I look, slave?" Nicole flashed me a smile. She was being coy. She knew how great she looked.

"You look soooo amazing Princess. I'm sure he'll love it."

Nicole smiled at me. She took a few minutes to put on a sexy shade of lipstick and other makeup.

"Okay, here's what is going to happen. I'm going to go out with Dan tonight...on your tab of course. You are to kneel at the foot of my bed until we arrive. Got it?"

"Yes Princess. I understand."

"Good. I'll see you in a few hours."

Nicole walked out after putting on a pair of three inch red heels.

Chapter 3

I waited by the foot of her bed for hours. She had left at 6:30 PM. It was now 9:30 PM and still no sign of Nicole. I really hated how she treated me, but I guess I didn't really have a choice in the matter.

I was really dreading the moment she and Dan walked through the doors. I was sure she would really humiliate me. Plus, I didn't want to see some other guy fuck Nicole. I mean I've been waiting months to fuck her and I probably never will. It just wasn't fair.

Soon enough I heard the jingle of keys near the door. The door opened and I heard Nicole giggling. She sounded slightly tipsy. I heard a deep voice as they walked towards the bedroom.

"So this is your place?" Dan said. "It's amazing."

"Wait till you see the bedroom."

Nicole led him into the bedroom where I was still kneeling.

The door opened and I saw Nicole, still in her beautiful

dress. Her date, Dan, was a large black man. Well, large was an understatement. He was 6'4" and towered over Nicole.

I'm not gay, but even I had to admit Dan was fucking handsome. He had his hair shaved and was wearing a very nice suit. He was well built too. You could see the outlines of his muscle as he took off his suit jacket. He hit the gym often, that's for sure.

"So is this that loser you were telling me about?"

"Yep, that's him."

"Haha yeah, he looks fucking pathetic. And what's that you have on his dick?"

"Oh this?" Nicole walked over and pulled me up by my chastity cage. "It's just a cage I keep him in. Keeps him nice and horny so he is very obedient. Isn't that right, slave?"

"Yes, Princess."

It was utterly humiliating the way she flaunted me around Dan. It really made me sick.

Dan laughed as Nicole waved my chastity cage around back and forth.

"So, slave...you have any idea what Dan and I are about to do?"

"Fuck?"

"Well, aren't you the smart one!"

"Get on your knees again and watch, bitch!"

"Yes, Princess."

Dan removed his shirt and pants while Nicole slipped off her dress. Nicole moved in and they began making out. I was so jealous. I couldn't even remember the last time Nicole and I made out. It was as far as I got with her in the bedroom.

I hear the sound of Nicole sucking on his lips. It looked and sounded so hot. My dick was getting hard in my cage already. I was thinking how good it would feel if Nicole had kissed me like that. She never kissed me like the way she was kissing Dan right now.

I could see the outline of Dan's hard dick in his boxers as he and Nicole made out on the bed. I could already tell he had a monster dick.

"I want you inside me, now!" Nicole moaned as Dan sucked on her neck. She removed her bra and panties, inviting him in to fuck her.

"You want my big black cock, don't you little slut?!" Dan bellowed. His voice echoed across the room.

"Yes! Please!"

Dan ripped off his boxers. He threw them on the floor right in front of where I was.

Wow....Dan was well endowed and that was an understatement. He was practically a horse from the waist down. I mean his dick must have been like 11 inches hard. I was only like four and a half when hard...he really did put me to shame.

Nicole grabbed his big dick and wrapped her lips around it.

Dan moaned in pleasure as she gave him the blowjob of his life.

"OMG your dick is so fucking huge! I love it!"

"Oh yeah!" Dan moaned. He grabbed the back of Nicole's head and rammed his dick into her throat while she choked. I was surprised he didn't kill her with his huge dick.

"I bet you wish I was sucking your little stupid dick like this, don't you slave?"

Nicole teased me as she licked the head of Dan's large dick.

"Yes, Princess. I wish it was me so bad."

"Well it's never going to be you. You're just a stupid slave. You'll never fuck me like a real man would."

To add insult to injury Nicole spat on my face. Her spit mixed with Dan's precum hit my nose as it rolled down to my mouth. It was utterly humiliating.

"Please fuck me, Dan. I want your dick in me so bad! I've

never had a dick as big as yours before! Please fuck me!"

I was so jealous of Dan. I've been begging Nicole to fuck me forever and this guy has her begging HIM for a fuck? What? The world was so cruel.

"You want this big black cock in your tiny pussy?!" Dan grabbed his dick and rubbed the tip all over Nicole's inflated pussy lips.

Nicole moaned even louder as Dan teased her. It was driving me crazy. I was just kneeling there at the foot of my bed with my locked up dick trying to get hard. Uggh.

"Alright, get ready babe! My big dick is going go fuck you!"

Dan slowly rammed his black dick into Nicole's tiny pussy. She moaned in pleasure as he fully inserted his horse-sized dick. I was pretty surprised he actually got it in there. Nicole was screaming in pleasure.

Dan stood up near the edge of the bed and grabbed Nicole by the knees. He used them to ram his dick even harder into Nicole.

By now, Nicole was screaming in pleasure. I was afraid the neighbors would hear her.

Dan didn't care though. He fucked her harder and harder.

"OMG! I forgot what it felt like to have a real man in me!"

Nicole was in heaven. I could only watch this horrid act in complete shame. I felt like such a loser. I wanted to fuck Nicole so bad. It was my worst nightmare having to watch Dan fuck the woman of my dreams.

"Fuck! Keep going! I'm going to cum!" Nicole announced.

"You're going to cum? Cum for me baby! Cum on my big black cock!!!"

Her body was convulsing as Dan picked up the pace of the fucking. Nicole screamed into her pillow as she came. I've never seen Nicole like that in my life. She loved it when Dan touched her. If only she would feel like that with me.

"God! Fuck me more Dan. I want more!"

"Beg me more slut!"

He picked up Nicole by the waist and flipped her on the bed so she was on her knees.

"Please Dan! Fuck me harder!"

"You got it babe."

Dan fucked Nicole from the back in true doggy fashion. I saw his large 11 inch dick ravage her tiny pussy. Oddly enough, I was fucking hard in my cage. In fact, precum dripped from my dick onto the floor.

It was like watching hot porn in real life. I hated how Dan was defiling the girl of my dreams, but the sex was hot. Even I couldn't deny that.

"OMG this feels so gooooood!" Nicole screamed at the top of her lungs. "If only my stupid slave was able to pleasure me like this!!"

"I'm sorry, Princess."

"Shut up! I don't want to hear your voice while I'm being pleasured!"

Wow...Nicole was really getting into the whole humiliation thing. God, I would have given anything to be Dan right now.

Dan forcibly flipped Nicole on her back. She laid back against the pillow while he fucked her in missionary.

I saw her toes clench as she had another orgasm. Dan's big black dick just continued to fuck her small and tight pussy. It must have felt so good. I could only dream about what it would feel like.

Nicole continued to scream in pleasure. "Suck on my toes, slave!"

"What?"

"I said suck on my toes while Dan fucks me! Do it or you'll regret it!"

Wow could this have been any more humiliating? I crawled over on my hands and knees to the bed and sucked on her right foot.

I saw Dan's big dick just ravage that pussy. It went in and out so quick. I sucked on her toes and she moaned in pleasure. I was still hard against my cage. I dreamed about how it was me instead of Dan.

"I'm going to cum!" Dan announced.

"Do it!! Please cum in me! I want your load!"

"Beg me you slut!!"

"Do it!!! Please!!" Nicole begged as she closed her eyes. "Keep sucking on my toes slave! Don't you dare stop!"

I sucked her toes like my life depended on it. I saw Dan's body convulse as he had the most amazing orgasm of his life.

"I'm cumming in your slut pussy!!!" Dan rammed his big black dick deeper and deeper into Nicole's pussy. I could tell the moment he came when Nicole screamed even louder.

"OMG that feels soooo good!!"

Dan collapsed on the bed on top of Nicole for a moment. Then he got up and pulled out.

"This was fun babe, but I've got to go. Need to get some work done tomorrow morning."

"Okay, babe." Nicole reached up and kissed Dan as he left. He gave me a look of pity as he left the room.

Nicole laid there in the bed for a few minutes, just relaxing from the after-sex glow.

"So, slave did you enjoy the show? Actually...I don't even need to ask. Look at how hard your dick is!"

Nicole was right. My dick was practically bursting out of the cage. My precum had dripped all the way to the tip of the cage.

"I have another surprise for you, slave."

I was beginning to hate all of Nicole's "surprises." She sat up on the bed and used her toes to tease my balls.

"You want to fuck me to bad, don't you? Like how Dan just fucked me?"

"Yes. Please, Princess. Please let me fuck you."

"You think this locked up dick deserves to fuck me?" Nicole clamped down on my right testicle with both feet, causing me to flinch in pain.

"No Princess, of course not."

"That's right, slave. All your dick is good for is to be locked up by me and to be abused whenever I feel like it. All you're good for is to serve me like a good boy."

"Yes, Princess. Anything you say."

"Good. Now, I want you to lick my pussy clean."

Nicole spread her legs as she leaned back. Dan's cum oozed out of her perfect pussy. Wow, there was a ton of his cum all over her.

I hesitated. It was so humiliating and I've never eaten cum before in my life.

"What's wrong, slave? You've begged so vigorously to eat my sweet pussy in the past."

"But it has Dan's cum all over it."

Nicole sat back up and slapped me in the face real hard. It was pretty painful. My cheek turned red instantly.

"That's right, you fucking bitch!! Dan's a real man. He gets to fuck me whenever he wants. You're just a fucking slave. The only way you will ever get to lick my pussy is if clean out his cum. Got it?! It better be clean."

"Yes, Princess. I am so sorry!" I begged for her forgiveness.

"Good, now lean in and clean me out."

Nicole spread her legs out again and I went in for it. I stuck my tongue out and tasted Dan's salty cum on my dream girl's pussy. I swallowed and it was the worst thing I've ever tasted in my life.

"How does it taste, slave?! Ha Ha Ha!!" Nicole couldn't hold back her laughter any longer.

"Disgusting Princess."

"Good. I'm glad. Now, lick the rest up or you'll be severely punished!!"

"Yes, my Princess."

I bowed my head down and cleaned Nicole's pussy of Dan's cum. It was the most humiliating thing in the world, but I didn't have a choice. After all, I was Nicole's Bitch Slave...

Taken In The Woods

Jessie Sinclair

Copyright © 2017 Jessie Sinclair

All Rights Reserved

The cool breeze of the Colorado mountain air brushed against our faces. Not a single cloud appeared in the sky. My wife, Kayla, and I were on a romantic getaway in the mountains. We had just arrived in our cabin for next week.

"Wow this place looks amazing!" Kayla said with a beautiful smile on her face.

I wrapped my hands around her. "Say...what do you say we have fun in the bedroom?" I brought my lips over and kissed her lightly on the back of the neck.

Kayla lightly slapped my hands away and turned around. "Oh stop it; we'll have plenty of time for that later. Don't you want to go check out some of the hiking trails?"

"Oh...um okay. Sure, let's go."

I was a bit disappointed. I had hoped that we would be able to start the weekend with a bang. You see...for the past two months Kayla and I have been kind of on a dry spell.

I mean when we first got married two years ago it was great; we had sex practically every night. However, as time went on, it seems we played less and less in the bedroom.

I guess wouldn't be such a big deal if we checked out some of the trails. I booked this cabin for the entire week, so it shouldn't be that hard to shack up with my own wife, right?

We exited the cabin; I waited near the front while Kayla walked to the reception desk insisting we get a map of the trails.

I was just walking around mindlessly and almost ran into two enormous black men. They must have been at least 6'5" and were very well built. Both were wearing tank tops and I could tell they were packing some real heat with their chiseled muscles.

"Oh sorry," one of them said as he nearly knocked me down. I didn't even get a word out before they walked in the other direction.

Kayla walked back from the office with two maps in her hands. The two black men graciously greeted her and she laughed with them.

Their brief exchange lasted all but a ten seconds; I wondered what they said to her. Did they hit on my wife?

"Hey, what did those guys say to you?" I anxiously asked her.

"Oh it was nothing; they asked it a pretty girl like me as lost."

"Oh okay. Well anyways, are you ready to head out?"

"Yeah, let's get going."

Kayla and I tried on of the easier trails since it was our first time hiking. It was incredibly beautiful outside. Lush, green forestry graced the horizon as began up the bumpy road.

Everything about being in nature with Kayla seemed to scream romance, yet I didn't get the same vibe from her. Oh well, it would only likely be a matter of time before she jumped my bones anyways.

After about a half hour of hiking, we decided to rest at the top of the road and to enjoy the scenery. I wrapped my arms around Kayla and kissed her on the cheek. She smiled back at me.

As I was about to say something I was interrupted by the two black men we saw earlier. This time they both had their shirts off.

"Hey didn't we see you guys earlier?" One of them said, his deep voice boomed with confidence.

Both of them were sporting ridiculously chiseled abs that would shame most men. I looked over and saw that Kayla checking them out!

"Oh yeah!" Kayla said, almost blushing. "I didn't catch your names."

"Oh I'm Deshawn and this is my friend, Jermaine."

Deshawn reached out his hand to shake my wife's. He kissed it like a gentleman while she blushed. The nerve of this guy! He obviously knew Kayla and I were together!

"Hi." Jermaine said with a smile on his face.

"Oh and this is my husband, Tony." She said patting me on the back.

"Tony, how are you doing?"

"Good." I said as I shook hands with each of them. Both men had a killer grip and I thought they would crush the bones in my hand like a gorilla would do to a coconut.

"So what brings you two to the mountains?"

"Oh we were just planning a weekend getaway," I said, "what about you two?"

"Oh we love hiking. We do all of the trails out here multiple times a year. We're professional long distance runners, so we love to train out here in the mountains."

"Wow that's pretty cool." Kayla said with a smile on her face.

"Hey it's going to get dark soon; you should head back to camp with us. Wouldn't want to get lost out here." Deshawn said.

"Oh okay. I think we just lost track of time." Kayla said.

We walked together with these two big black men. They seemed nice and cool on the outside, but I had a weird feeling about them. I didn't like how they flirted with Kayla right in front of my face.

It seemed both men were trying their best to flex their muscles and crack jokes. It was a bit unsettling in my book.

We finally made it back to camp.

"Say...you two want to join us for a little camp out?" Jermaine asked us.

"Well, I don't know we already paid for our cabin and we don't exactly have a tent." I said. The truth was I didn't want to spend another minute with these guys. I just wanted to take Kayla back to our room and have a little fun.

"You sure? We've got s'mores, beer, and a bonfire."

"Oh come on Tony, are you scared of the dark?" My wife teased me.

"Okay okay, let's do it."

The four of us walked back to their campsite. It was a large luxurious tent around a fire pit. Deshawn started a fire pretty quickly. We sat around the fire, as Jermaine went inside the tent.

"Hope you two are hungry for s'mores." Deshawn teased. We began warming up marshmallows over the fire to start the process.

I wrapped my arm around Kayla and she leaned her head over. Damn I couldn't believe I was spending time with these two guys instead of fucking my wife.

"Hey, you said you had beers right?"

"Sure do." Deshawn said as he picked one out of the cooler for me.

"Thanks."

If I was going to be stuck here, I might as well have a

drink to ease the mood.

Before long, Jermaine came back out and sat with us. He
pulled out a blunt of weed. "You guys mind?" He said looking
back at us.

"Oh it's no problem, go ahead." I said.

Jermaine lit it up and smoked his marijuana. Deshawn also
took a few hits as both men were talking to Kayla about their
travel adventures.

It was almost immediately when I smelled the familiar scent
of weed. My wife and I hadn't done any since college. This batch
smelled particularly strong.

"Wow that smells like some powerful stuff." I said, waving
my hand around my nose for emphasis.

"Oh, it's a special home brew. Great for athletes!" Deshawn
said.

"Is that so?" Kayla seemed interest all of a sudden.

"Oh, it's VERY true." Jermaine took another puff of the blunt.

"Well what's so special about it? Let me take a hit!"

"Well, we should let you know that this is not for beginners. It's very powerful stuff."

Kayla didn't seem fazed.

"Well let me try first then." I said sticking out my palm.

Jermaine handed me the cigar and I took a quick puff. It was strong, but nothing I hadn't experienced in the past.

"It's not so bad." I handed it back to him, trying to sound macho in front of my wife as sat next to these two muscular black men. I took another sip of my beer.

"I meant it's very strong for women."

"And what do you mean by that?" Kayla seemed to take offense to what they said.

"Let's just say the weed makes women more suggestive to ideas." Deshawn replied.

"Yeah, right. Let me take a hit."

"We're just warning you." He teased. There they were again...flirting with my wife.

"Just give it to me."

I don't know if it was the weed, but I was actually enjoying the playful banter between my wife and these two black men.

Kayla took a hit of their special mix and nothing appeared to happen at first so she took another hit.

"How do you feel?" I asked her.

"Whoa..." She said in somewhat of a daze. "That was some strong stuff."

A few moments later, I was feeling almost hypnotized and a bit tired. I guess it was drinking the beer on an empty stomach...no that couldn't, be it right?

"Wow! Did you see the big hit she just took?" Deshawn asked his friend. Jermaine nodded while smiling.

All of a sudden Kayla put her hands on Jermaine's chest. She rubbed her hands around, feeling every square inch of his muscles.

"Wow, you're soooo muscular." She said in a sultry voice.

Was my wife coming onto this black guy?

"I bet you want to kiss me now, you whore." His voice was entirely dominant.

"I want to kiss you." She repeated after him.

Kayla wrapped her hands around his neck and leaned in for a passionate kiss. I watched my wife lock lips with this handsome black man in front of me.

Meanwhile Deshawn clapped. "I told you! It was powerful stuff!"

"What do you mean?" I said.

"Well...our weed makes white girls crave...chocolate."

"It does what?!"

I regretted letting Kayla try it.

Kayla was in the middle of a hot make out session with
Jermaine. I didn't know if it was the weed or the beer, but I
was feeling pretty weak.

"Hey...what did you guys put in this beer?"

"Oh it was nothing, just a little sedative so you can enjoy
the show." Deshawn said in a calm voice.

A sedative? Those guys set us up! They saw Kayla flirting
with them and now they were about to have their way with her.

"I want to see your cocks." Kayla said with a devious smile
on her face.

Deshawn and Jermaine looked at each other and smiled. They stood up and dropped their shorts to the floor. Meanwhile I was too tired to even get up. All I was able to do was watch in horror...and a little excitement at what was to come.

Kayla dropped to her knees in front of these naked black guys. Both of them had huge horse cocks...they were both at least nine inches and thick.

"This little whore wants to suck our cocks, right?"

"Yes, please let me suck on your cocks." She begged.

I couldn't believe what I was hearing! The sedative already kicked in so I was too tired to do anything.

"What are you talking about, Kayla?"

My wife made eye contact with me. "I haven't been satisfied with you for some time," she said, "I need their big black cock to make me cum."

She began sucking on Jermaine's cock. She wrapped her lips around the head and sucked. Her tongue flicked around in a masterful performance. Jermaine jerked his head back as he was being pleasured by my wife.

Deshawn go on the ground behind Kayla and placed the tip of his cock right on her pussy. He teased her by rubbing it around her clit.

Kayla moaned into Jermaine's cock. I couldn't believe my wife was going to be used by these big black men as a sex toy. Deshawn inserted his cock into her pussy until his balls touched her ass.

"Oh god!" My wife moaned. "You guys are SO BIG!"

"Man this whore can't get enough of black dick! Ha Ha" Jermaine laughed.

He grabbed the back of Kayla's head and fucked her senseless. With every thrust, his balls collided with her chin. Kayla gagged on his large member.

Deshawn picked up the speed from behind. Kayla moaned in pleasure. The weed was making her crave black cock so bad.

"Oh! Mhhh! Mhhh!"

"How tight is that white pussy?"

"It's the tightest I ever had!"

For some reason, I was getting really turned on by these black guys using my wife as a toy. It was probably the weed, but I was getting hard in my pants. I never experienced anything like it.

"You want my cum on your face?"

"Yes! Please! Yes! I want your cum on my face!"

We were being pretty loud. I was afraid other campers would come see what the commotion was all about.

"I love how this bitch begs!" Jermaine laughed.

Deshawn inserted is cock all the way so his balls rested against Kayla's ass. He wanted to watch the fireworks his friend was about to show off.

Jermaine grabbed the back of her head again and rammed his cock in and out like lightning. Kayla took it like a champ. I was regaining control of my limbs, but for some reason I had no desire to stop this incredible scene.

"Oh I've never felt a better tongue in my life!"

Jermaine jerked his head back as his eyes rolled to the sky. "Oh God! Yes!"

I saw his muscles tighten up.

"Ready for my cum?!"

Kayla nodded in obedience. She wanted that cum and I wanted to see him mark my wife as his territory.

"Here it comes you whore!!"

Jermaine pulled his cock out of Kayla's mouth. An audible pop could be heard; then he let it all loose. His cock erupted all over her face.

I saw wave after wave of cum coat my wife. His cum shot

into her eyes, on her lips, and all over her nose.

I finally regained the use of my arms and legs. I moved to position myself closer to the action. I was inches away from my wife's face as Jermaine's orgasm finally subsided.

"How did you enjoy that, you slut?"

Kayla opened her eyes as the cum flowed down the side of her face. "Oh god, it's so warm. That was so amazing!"

I couldn't have agreed more. I'm sure it was the marijuana talking, but I was rock hard in my pants.

Seeing as his friend was finally finished, Deshawn began fucking Kayla gain.

Meanwhile, Jermaine lit up another blunt of weed. The scent made Kayla and I go crazy.

Kayla moaned louder and louder. "Oh my god! You're so fucking huge! Fuck me harder!"

I looked at the cum dripping down my wife's face. It hadn't

dried yet and looked like someone had put sunscreen all over her.

"Why don't you kiss your husband?" Jermaine said as he sat back down on the log with his feet up. He took another hit of the cigar.

Kayla moved her face up and we made eye contact in the midst of this erotic scene. We locked lips and smeared Jermaine's cum all over. I tasted her tongue. It was a bitter flavor; I guess that's what black dick tasted like.

I felt Kayla's tongue dart around in my mouth as Deshawn picked up the speed. He was really going at it hard.

"Oh god, I want to fuck your ass you white whore!"

Deshawn exited her pussy and placed his cock on top of her asshole.

"Ready for this?"

Kayla looked at me, unsure of herself. I looked her in the eyes and nodded for my approval.

"Yes, I'm ready!" She said, anticipating the pain that was about to come.

"Here I go!" Deshawn announced.

He inserted his cock into her ass. Luckily it was already lubed up from her pussy juices. Deshawn wasn't gentle at all. He went in as fast as he could.

Kayla moaned in a mixture of pain and pleasure. I held on to her hands as this big black man defiled her ass.

"Wow this bitch can sure take it in the ass." Jermaine remarked as he took another puff of his weed. The scent reached our nostrils as we all became high at the same time.

"Oh god! Go faster!" Kayla screamed. If anyone was outside they surely heard her screams.

Deshawn grabbed my wife's waist with his giant gorilla hands. He rammed his cock into her ass faster and faster. His balls slammed against her pussy, teasing her with a bit of pleasure.

"Oh Deshawn, I want your hot cum in me!"

"Yeah? You're going to get it then!"

I sat back for a moment, allowing Kayla to enjoy the moment. Jermaine gave me a puff of this incredible weed as I watched everything unfold.

"Here's my cum in your ass, whore!"

Deshawn erupted in her ass.

"Oh! There's so much! It's so warm!"

"Mhhg!" Deshawn grunted and moaned as he filled my wife up.

When he finally took his cock out, his cum leaked down to her pussy.

"Oh god, you got some sweet pussy and ass, bitch!" He remarked.

Deshawn walked over to his friend and took a hit of the

weed and sighed.

"Whew, that was amazing!" Jermaine exclaimed.

I couldn't have agreed more. My cock was dripping wet in my pants as I watched these two big black men devour my wife and all of her holes.

"Oh god, I've never experienced anything so amazing." Kayla said while panting like a dog. "You were right...that weed is something else."

Even though Kayla was just fucked by those black men, I wanted to have her to myself again.

"Hey you guys mind if I borrow that weed?"

"Oh not at all...take some." Jermaine handed me a cigar.

I thanked the guys and helped Kayla back to our cabin for some more fun. We fucked for hours that night and it was all because of Jermaine and Deshawn. It wouldn't be the last time we would see those two big black men on our weekend getaway as well...

Made in the USA
Monee, IL
25 November 2022

18507304R00157